FAREWELL TO TEXAS

Texas wasn't big enough for gambler and gunfighter Rogate "Rogue" Bishop and he thought he ought to move along. He figured Mexico, some three hundred miles off, was his shortest jump out of Texas.

On the way, despite hearing that the Texas Rangers have him on their list, when trouble explodes at the Hatchet Ranch, the temptation for one last troubleshooting job proves too great. The owner's daughter is missing and Rogue is after a handsome reward for bringing her back to her father, Simon Dyal. Before long, the blast of six-guns rips across the valley!

FAREWELL TO TEXAS

L. L. Foreman

GUNSMOKE

This hardback edition 2008
by BBC Audiobooks Ltd
by arrangement with
Golden West Literary Agency

ISBN 978 1 405 68231 2

British Library Cataloguing in Publication Data available.

Printed and bound in Great Britain by
CPI Antony Rowe, Chippenham, Wiltshire

ONE

Like many another uncurbed Texas locality, Cedar Valley developed serious symptoms of respectability after the smoke cleared, the damage was tallied up, and law and order came shouldering in with all the excessive zeal of a bustling latecomer. Its reforming fever ran the full course.

It slammed the door on gunhands and hardcases, cut them off the payrolls, and served them notice to move on.

They had come by invitation and enjoyed a warm hospitality while the range war lasted, but the light of peace exposed them as undesirable. They moved on, money spent, credit gone, the law grown so deplorably tight that a Saturday rider could get jailed for putting his horse to the boardwalk and sky-shooting, or some such whimsey.

Cedar Valley even turned its newly righteous face away from the man who was largely responsible for nailing down the trouble and paving the way for peace.

He had known that the success of his efforts would end his usefulness here—that he'd work himself out of a job, as always happened. The pushing group of big cattlemen had finally pulled back to their own range, his name on their black books. The small ranchers who, hard-pressed, had hired him to head their fight, could sleep these nights with both eyes shut and dream rosy dreams of a rising beef market.

What he had not foreseen was that his welcome would wear out.

He had never before stayed on anywhere, once the job was finished, and he was growing dissatisfied with a fly-by-night way of living. A man ought to settle down somewhere along the line. Pick a place where he could let himself loosen. Give his sharp vigilance a rest. Sink roots.

But the soil wasn't right for the likes of him. In the fair foliage of Cedar Valley he was poison oak. Dake Hession, a leader among the small ranchers, finally got up the nerve to bring it into the open, emboldened by a few drinks and the

5

near presence of friends who were criticising the new wooden horse outside Cluett's Saddle Shop.

"I'll tell you straight how it is, Mr. Bishop."

They still addressed him with careful respect. He was Mr. Rogate Bishop and only in the heat of emergencies, now past, had they ever dropped the Mr. They all knew his nickname, but didn't use it in his hearing. They hadn't got close enough to him, and never would.

"You're too dangerous to know," Dake Hession said. He was an elderly man who believed that his age conferred wisdom and granted him ponderous authority. Savoring the phrase, he repeated it. "Too dangerous to know! If you stay round here it'll burr the big fellers. They'll think we're up to something!"

"You worry what they think?"

The group at the saddler's wooden horse went on gazing at it. Not talking. Listening.

Dake Hession raised a hand. "Wait, there's more. If one of us was to hire you—me, say. If I was to take you on to ramrod my outfit, my friends'd think *I* was up to something! See how it is, Mr. Bishop?"

Mr. Bishop observed dryly that friendship and trust among them seemed to leave a good deal to be desired. "It wasn't in my mind to hire out. Running somebody's two-bit spread's not exactly my game."

Among the group, Joel Sumpter, a neighbor of Hession's, swung slowly around. Giving up further pretense of inspecting the wooden horse, the group turned with him. Sumpter spoke, evidently talking for the rest of them, eager to take it up from Hession.

"We know your game! We don't like it!" Where Hession stood on his age for prestige, Sumpter depended on his large size and flaming temper. Throughout the trouble he had proved as hard to control as a wild bull. "We don't want Rogue Bishop—"

"Now, Joel—!" Hession began.

Sumpter waved him aside. "Ain't that who he is? I say it plain out! Rogue Bishop, gunfighter and gambler!"

So. Thurman must have talked in the Star. Bishop said temperately, "You've got it backward. Gambling's my first game. Troubleshooting's my second string. A gun can come in handy for both."

"The trouble here's all past. Don't owe you anything, do we?"

"Just your outfits."

"We paid you for what you done! Plenty!"

"Too much?"

"Plenty, I said!"

"Well, now," one of the men put in, "he spent a lot on—"

"We didn't take on to pay his expenses too!"

Cluett came out of his shop to lace a saddle on the wooden horse for display, the better to listen in. Men emerged inquisitively from the Star, and others paused along the street. With a gallery to play up to, Joel Sumpter couldn't resist making a grand flourish. From the first he had resented taking orders from an outsider, deeming himself capable of leadership, and it went against his grain to give respect to the man he regarded as a hired gun boss. The memory of past politenesses still rankled in him. Now the mildness of Bishop's manner encouraged him to insult the man. Digging a wad of bills from his pocket, he peeled off one and thrust it at him.

"If you're broke, gunman—here!"

There were some murmurs of protest, some muffled snickers. Then, abruptly, silence. The look in Bishop's eyes was enough to freeze the marrow of anybody but a blindfolded fool, and the onlookers once more saw Bishop as the thunderbolt that shattered their enemies.

He stood tall and somber in his knee-length black coat and wide-brimmed black hat. At first glance he bore some resemblance to an archdeacon severely inspecting the paths of profligacy, for his was the decent garb of a dwindling breed of men: hard-living men who followed their hazardous trade with a flair for style and a touch of dignity. A second glance brought the distinct impression that he inspected those wayward paths for his own personal benefit. His sun-darkened face normally had the sardonic humor of a pagan god, and his deep-set gray eyes reflected a casual cynicism that also was not without humor.

His humor vanished now. He performed two swift motions as one, his left hand batting the bill and the fingers holding it, his right fetching Sumpter a pistol-crack slap in the face that sent the rancher reeling half-around.

It wasn't only the insult of the proffered bill that angered Bishop—it was the slander of calling him a gunman. He liked to think that there was a distinction between gunfighter and gunman, as between a high-grade gambler and a tinhorn. The distinction sometimes wore pretty thin, but it was there and it wasn't for any loud-mouthed cowman to ignore it.

Dake Hession spread his hands in dismay, and the group in front of Cluett's Saddle Shop took on grim looks. Sumpter wasn't any too popular, but he was a Cedar Valley man, one of them, and Bishop himself had impressed upon them the necessity of presenting a solid front.

Sumpter righted himself, shaking his head to clear it from that ringing slap and working his hurt fingers. He glared at Bishop. Seeing that no gun was coming up, he rushed at him, his massive arms swinging. Bishop crouched forward and met him with a straight-arm blow to the mouth, stopping him dead, and the group muttered. Sumpter dabbed his smashed mouth with the back of his hand. He stared wildly at the blood and charged again like a madman. Bishop's next punch threw him off-stride to stumble on his high heels, and he bellowed, "God damn you, I'll—!"

"Quit it, Sumpter!" Bishop said. "Quit it, or I'll break you!"

"The hell!"

Somebody in the group sang out: "The hell he will, Joel! Take him—you can do it!"

Bishop drew a breath and went in for the kill. He slammed his man and straightened him up, followed through with a slashing uppercut, then drove on to the midriff. Sumpter bowed low, gasping, keeping to his feet. The group automatically started forward, evidently to pitch in and save him from a murderous mauling, for Bishop had stepped to him and had his hands ready as if to grab his ears and knee him in the face.

Having no such intention, Bishop placed both hands on Sumpter's hanging head and shoved. Sumpter barged backward into the group and on through, carrying two or three floundering along with him, and Cluett let out a yell as his new wooden horse and new saddle toppled over and crashed through the front window of his shop.

At that moment U. S. Marshal Harley reached the scene, his gun drawn to discourage anyone else from doing likewise.

Afterward, when Bishop had paid Cluett for the window, U. S. Marshal Harley discussed the prospects for lasting peace. "The odds are against it," he said, "as long as you're here!"

He was a neat, compactly built man of crisply direct speech, who had headed the law invasion of Cedar Valley and was staying on until he made certain that the law wouldn't shake loose.

"In fact," he added thoughtfully, "the odds are against peace anywhere you light, from all I hear. I guess it's natural, though. You're a troubleshooter. You go where there's trouble."

It was only partly true, but Bishop didn't trouble to deny it. He drew out a cigar and nipped off its end. This Cedar Valley affair, he mentioned, was his last job. "I figured on settling here, Marshal."

Harley nodded. "I know about the poker table you aimed to set up in the Star. Everybody knows. Thurman spoke of it." Thurman owned the Star—a good saloon which could be greatly improved, in Bishop's opinion, by organizing its gambling under his expert hand. "It won't do!" Harley said.

"You object?"

"*They* object! Cedar Valley ought to prosper now the trouble's over. You're out to drain off their spare money into your pocket, right?"

"Only enough to buy myself a spread here."

"They won't have it!"

Bishop forcefully expelled a spear of cigar smoke. "Damned ingrates!" he growled.

Harley permitted himself a rare grin, quickly erased. "I see it their way. You spell trouble, even if you don't intend it, and they've had a bellyful. You see what happened today. They're ready to turn against you."

"Texas cowmen!"

"With them it's a case of—well—self-preservation. They've got peace and they want to keep it. They see you as a danger to the peace. Your job's done." Harley paused. "Do me the favor to quit Cedar Valley, will you?"

Bishop scanned briefly the lawman's face. "A favor to you?"

"I'm staying here till you go," Harley told him simply.

Bishop took the cigar from between his teeth and studied it for a long time. "All right," he said finally, harshly, "I'll get out!"

Harley nodded, gazing off. "I return the favor. Watch out for Rangers. They've got the name of Rogue Bishop on their list. I don't recall for what. Danger to peace, maybe."

"Texas," said Bishop, "is getting so peace-loving, hell wouldn't have it, hm? So I'll get out of Texas!"

"She's a big ol' country to get out of."

"Big and bigoted, yeah!"

He got his horse from the livery, settled his bills, and left Cedar Valley without any goodbyes. To hell with Cedar Valley. To hell with Texas. Not long ago it had been a fine broad land of free-living men, self-reliant men with the fighting edge, tolerant of any indiscretion except the shameful wrong of running to the aw. Now it was all laid out and tied down, and lawmen commonly went nosing into other people's business. A sour state of affairs.

The thought came to him that perhaps he was a little outside of the changing times. There weren't many places left where he could afford to put his feet up and relax. Not this side of Mexico, anyway.

Mexico, he mused. Things didn't change down there. The people there regarded change with deep suspicion. They sensibly kept law to a minimum, and shrugged off the ridiculous notion of holding last year's misdeeds against a man.

Also, Mexico was his shortest jump out of Texas. A jump of some three hundred miles, he estimated. And watch out for the Rangers. Damned busybodies. His thoughts harked back to the wry disappointment behind him: Cedar Valley, the last of many troubleshooting jobs. The very last. He sighed shortly and rode on.

TWO

His slanting route down the boot of Texas took him skirting past the little rivers and fine grasslands and timber of what was loosely called the Hill Country by its inhabitants. In the gone days it had been Comanche country—the Comanches had a strong liking for regions that were hard to get at and they fought long to keep this one. It lay only seventy miles north of San Antonio, but could have been on the other side of the world for all that it resembled most of the rest of Texas. No flat prairies. No blinding dust. Green grass. Due to the high terrain, even its climate was different.

Also its people, Bishop observed as he rode into the little stone town that bore the Teutonic name of Fredericksburg. He knew of this place from hearsay, and seeing it for the first time he could understand why men wagged their heads when speaking of it. It seemed unreal, an affront to common sense, a mirage. It decidedly wasn't Texas, nor even tolerably American.

The square houses of quarried stone crowded close to the street. They had outside staircases leading up to attics, and steep roofs that sloped high in front. A larger one had round-topped windows and double doors sunk deeply into the thick walls, and another appeared to be built in the form of a ship. There were signs here and there, all in German. A couple of church spires pointed spindly fingers to heaven. There was no noise. It was Sunday.

Bishop hailed a man in the street. "Got a hotel in this town?"

The man wore thick homemade clothes and his gait wasn't that of a horseman. He blinked earnestly as if stumped by a knotty problem, gazing blue-eyed at Bishop's mouth.

Bishop tried again. "Livery stable? Saloon?"

The blue eyes hardened. The man trudged on. Bishop frowned after him. "You'd think," he muttered, "they'd been here long enough to know American." Their isolation was the answer, he guessed. That and their close clannishness. Or maybe the man just plain didn't like his looks.

11

He spoke to two men and a woman who were hurrying by, altering his curtness to a more polite request because of the woman. "Could you kindly point me out the hotel?" They sent him blank stares and hastened on in the direction of the spindly church spires. He silently damned the town of Fredericksburg.

A voice called to him, "They do not love a Texan!" It came from a man standing in the deep doorway of the house with the round-topped windows. He was tall, as tall as Bishop, but skeleton-thin.

"Nor me, right now," Bishop responded, "but I'll steer a Texan to a drink."

· "And so will I. Come in!"

"Be right with you!"

The house, Bishop learned, was the Kiehne House, and while it wasn't precisely a saloon, it did have a drinking room furnished with tables and benches and rows of beer tankards. His host gave his name only as Karl.

"Beer? We brew our own. Good German beer."

"Whiskey if you've got it. Have one with me?"

"Delighted!"

They drank. "Pretty quiet town, Karl."

"Sunday. Everybody goes to church."

"Not you?"

Karl smiled. The smile made his face more cadaverous, with its high-bridged narrow nose and thin lips. He used the somewhat stilted English of an educated foreigner who didn't have many opportunities to exercise it, and evidently he welcomed Bishop's company.

"The pastor quarreled with me on a point of theology and called me a heretic. He will beg me back to the fold again soon, as I have a wasting ailment and he worries for my soul, but meantime I am letting him—how do you say?—stew, yes."

"What's the grudge against Texans here?" Bishop asked, and Karl replied that it went back over a period of years.

Fredericksburg, he said, was named in honor of Frederick the Great of Prussia, who never did a thing for it in return. It was founded by German settlers who moved to the locality under the auspices of the Adelsverein—the Society for the Protection of German Immigrants in Texas. The good Lord knew they needed all the protection they could get in those days, from Comanche raids, devastating epidemics, famines, and Texans who despised foreign-talking farmers.

During the War between the States—the Rebellion, Karl

12

called it—his people caught hell for staying out of it. The men took to the hills rather than serve in the Confederate Army, and were hunted like outlaws. A party of them, trying to escape to Mexico, were slaughtered by Texas troops, on the principle that any man so debased as to refuse to fight for Texas and the South deserved killing.

"No, my people do not love Texans!" Karl concluded. "They will have nothing to do with them, nor even speak their language. True, the English language is not confined to Texas—scarcely so! But that means nothing to my people. They are very much isolated here, very narrow in the mind. Having suffered Texan persecution, they say, 'Shun the Texans!' "

"Sometimes," Bishop remarked, "I could drink to that myself."

Taking the hint, Karl refilled the glasses. Spots of color were mounting to his emaciated cheeks. His speech grew more rapid and fluent.

"I will give you an instance of my people's attitude. Last month a young lady went missing. Her name is Kerry Dyal. She is the daughter of Simon Dyal. You know of him?"

Bishop shook his head, and Karl raised his eyebrows in apparent surprise.

"Simon Dyal owns an immense ranch farther up in the Hill Country. A group of ranches, rather, all run under his Hatchet Brand. Cattle. A rich man."

"I've heard of the Hatchet outfit."

"I would think it strange if you hadn't. Kerry Dyal is believed to have been abducted—kidnaped for ransom. Simon Dyal has twice paid ransom demands for her return. She remains missing. Her whereabouts is unknown. It is feared that she is no longer alive, probably buried in some lonely arroyo."

"Where does it concern you and your people?"

Karl's smile again cracked his face. "We think the young lady left home of her own free will, for some reason known to herself—possibly a romantic reason."

"What makes you think that?"

"Several days before she went missing, a Mexican gentleman arrived here. In most places he would not have aroused any curiosity, perhaps, but this is Fredericksburg. Like you, he was conspicuous. As out of place here, as they say, as a pistol in the pulpit. With him was a woman, a peon woman of middle age, a sort of servant. They came in a surrey, of all

13

things. He must have rented it in San Antonio—nowhere nearer could he have obtained such an elegant equipage. They put up at the Nimitz, the stone ship down the street. He came in here quite often. I had a white wine which pleased his taste. Oh, he was a gentleman of discrimination! And handsome as the devil. We liked him—he was not a Texan!"

"Maybe he was a Tejano," Bishop suggested.

Karl shook his head. "No, a Mexican. And very much the hidalgo. He had manners most polished. He rented a horse and rode off on long trips up into the hills. When at last he left here for good, it was at night—and in his San Antonio surrey with him were seen not one woman, but two! The second one was dressed like the servant woman, shawled to the eyes, and her head covered. Still, her youthfulness could not be hidden. Next day we learned of the abduction of Simon Dyal's daughter. Abduction, indeed! She went without the slightest struggle!"

"She could've been drugged," Bishop said. His mind, almost despite himself, picked alertly at possibilities.

"She did not act drugged. The impression was that she fled willingly with the handsome hidalgo and his woman servant." Karl raised a bony finger. "My point is, we kept our mouths shut. Why should we run to Simon Dyal with this knowledge? No, no—let the damned Texans stew! There you have the attitude of my people. It is amusing, h'n?"

Bishop nodded slowly. "It's something! The girl runs off with a Mexican, and the rascal bites her father for two ransom payments and still keeps hold of her! Doesn't Simon Dyal have any idea at all about how she left?"

"Obviously not," Karl replied. "It is taken for granted that she was kidnaped by a gang. She went out for an afternoon ride and never returned. Her horse was found next day tethered to a tree. On the ground were signs of a scuffle. Pinned to the saddle was a note, warning that the girl would be killed instantly if there was any attempt at pursuit. Oh, a clever man was Herr Risa!"

Bishop's fingers tightened abruptly on his whiskey glass. "What name did you say?"

"Risa. In Spanish it means 'laughter,' does it not? It suited him, after a fashion. Herr Risa had a ready smile. It had a merry wickedness in it." Karl rose from the table. "Now I must prepare for the Sunday rush. Our pastor's dry sermons give them a mighty thirst for beer!"

Bishop sat on, sunk in meditation. Common sense urged

him to quit Texas by the shortest route. If Marshal Harley had told the truth and the Texas Rangers had him on their list, the sensible thing was to follow his wish and head for Mexico.

Yet here, all unexpectedly—here in this freakish little German town—came opportunity, dropped right in his lap. One last troubleshooting job. Hunting for a missing girl was considerably out of his line, but it promised payment and he could use the money. Simon Dyal had paid two ransoms; he'd pay a reward for her return. If she still lived. Some question there. No certainty that the young woman who left with Risa was Dyal's daughter. Could have been anybody, a Mexican girl.

Risa. Ricardo de Risa. Bishop pondered over Karl's description of him. It certainly fitted that black-hearted, sharp-witted, faithless pistolero of old acquaintance.

The pealing of church bells brought him to his feet. "Karl, how do I get to Hatchet?"

"Go northwest and you will strike a road to Forks—a little cowtown where anyone will direct you to Dyal's home ranch, the headquarters. But why? To tell him what I have told you? You don't owe him that favor!"

"No—doing myself a favor," Bishop said. "Or am I?"

The same question recurred forcibly to him at the Hatchet headquarters.

"So you're Bishop, are you?" Simon Dyal snapped in a challenging tone. "Rogue Bishop, the hell-raiser who sided against some friends of mine up in the Cedar Valley country!"

Bishop nodded. It was a bad beginning.

Simon Dyal was a short, thick-built man, quite old. He wore a wrinkled suit, the baggy pants making his legs appear squatty, the vest held by one strained button over his heavy chest. He was ugly, his skin brown-stained and scarred like a withered apple, his mouth belligerent with a sideways twist and thick lower lip. His right eye was bloodshot and he kept the lid half shut. He hadn't offered Bishop the hospitality of his house; they stood in the yard. Several of the ranch hands lounged in the shade of the bunkhouse. Three or four of them Bishop judged to be hardcases. They looked tougher than the ordinary run of punchers.

"What makes you think you might find my daughter?" Dyal demanded.

His rough tone brought a glint to Bishop's eyes, but he

15

answered evenly, "I've got a hunch I know the man who took her."

"Men, you mean! You come at the right time. The county sheriff's here!" Dyal turned his head and called to the house, "Sutter! Here's Rogue Bishop telling me he knows who took my daughter!"

County Sheriff Sutter came out, followed by a younger man whose garb and pale shade of skin marked him as anything but a man of the range. The white shirt and flat-heeled boots looked oddly out of place. Sutter, a rock-faced man in his middle years, confronted Bishop and eyed him up and down quickly.

"All right, speak up! What can you tell me?"

"Not a damn thing!" Bishop said. "My business is with Dyal."

The young man in the white shirt inserted himself. "Business?" His gaze searched Bishop's face, and Bishop saw in his light eyes a good deal of shrewdness and purposeful strength. "Perhaps I'm the one you should talk to." His accent was that of a Southerner.

"Who are you?"

"Frank Wittrock." Dyal answered for him. "My business manager."

"I'm not dealing with go-betweens," Bishop told the Hatchet owner. "You're the girl's father. I've an idea I may be able to track her down. I'm offering to try."

"For a price?"

"Name it! I hear you've already paid out two ransoms."

"Five thousand each. I'll pay no more till my daughter is delivered safe to me. Not a penny!"

"That's agreed. Five thousand if I bring her back?"

Before Dyal could reply, Frank Wittrock broke in again. "You seem to know a good deal about the affair, more than we do! Speaking of go-betweens, is this an attempt to collect another ransom? Do you come from the kidnap gang?"

Bishop looked at him. "Young fella, your tongue's too loose!" He shot out a hand and grasped the front of the white shirt. "Bridle it!"

Frank Wittrock, making no move to pull loose, cocked his fair head to glance beyond Bishop. Besides shrewdness and force, his eyes now contained flash of cool nerve. They were not young eyes.

"None of that!" Simon Dyal struck at Bishop's arm. Bishop fended the blow with a twist of his elbow, and Dyal winced.

16

Then County Sheriff Sutter barked a name. "Osterberg! Back off! I'm handling this! Bishop, turn Wittrock loose!"

Bishop released his grip on the white shirt of the Southerner, and wheeled slowly around. He met the staring round eyes of the man Sutter had spoken to, milky brown eyes circled by muddy whites. " 'Lo, Owl," he said. "Haven't met you since—let's see now—Piedras Negras, wasn't it?"

Owl Osterberg didn't return the greeting, nor did his staring eyes waver. A step to his rear stood three men. Bishop checked into his memory for their names. Jay Nunn. Eben Dekker. Colorado George. The men at the bunkhouse had risen to their feet. He spoke to Owl Osterberg again. "You heard what the sheriff said!" He watched while Osterberg and the trio moved back, and turned to Sutter. "Your deputies?" he asked, and the county sheriff shook his head.

Frank Wittrock, tucking in his crumpled white shirt, answered, "Osterberg is the range boss. A good loyal man."

"And tough!" Bishop commented. He had known Osterberg and the three others some years ago when their activities kept them close to the Mexican border. Any outfit they rode for was expecting trouble or preparing to make it. "How about giving me a description of your daughter, Dyal?"

Simon Dyal eyed him glaringly for a minute. "Come in the house." He stumped to it, Bishop behind him, Sutter and Wittrock following.

For the home of a wealthy cattleman whose diverse ranching interest covered half of the Hill Country, Simon Dyal's house was as barren of comfort as a barracks. Large, two-storied with high ceilings and tall windows, it was a mansion that had become mainly the working headquarters of a sprawling ranch. Downstairs the bare and dusty floors gave off hollow echoes to the rap of hard heels, and uncarpeted stairs led gloomily up to what Bishop supposed would be the living quarters, such as they were. There was no sign of a woman's touch anywhere, no curtains at the windows, and a glimpse of the kitchen showed it to be a nest presided over by a sour-faced cripple, obviously an ex-cowpuncher.

The main room downstairs, intended for a spacious living room, was outfitted as an office. It held two desks and some wooden filing cases. This apparently was Frank Wittrock's province, as business manager. The fireplace needed shoveling out, and cordwood was stacked carelessly on the floor. It was as if Simon Dyal had deliberately abused this fine house of his, defiled it, stripped it of all refinements and wantonly encouraged its ruin.

And yet, above the fireplace hung a painting in a gilt frame, the portrait of a girl. It was incongruous, the one bit of color and elegance, as eye-catching as a jewel. "My daughter," Dyal grunted, gesturing at it, and he fastened his good eye on Bishop as if watchful to catch a betraying reaction of recognition.

"Does it look like her?"

"Yes." Dyal raised his eye to it. A pause, and he said, "Her mother painted it two years ago."

"Pretty girl," Bishop said, gazing at it. "More'n pretty." He didn't think he'd have any trouble remembering that face.

Dyal made no reply. Frank Wittrock and the county sheriff stood silent, their eyes shuttling between Bishop and the picture.

He felt that the picture had been painted with much loving care. Perhaps it flattered the girl, for it showed a flawless complexion and what he suspected might possibly be too-perfect features, but the girl's mother had managed to put in something about the eyes that made the face more arresting than merely beautiful. Dark blue eyes, broodingly serious, with a faint slant that gave them an odd look of skeptical inquiry, of disbelieving what they saw. The eyebrows were dark wings, and above an ivory forehead the dark hair, parted in the middle, was swept back to repeat the pattern of the eyebrows. Not a face to forget.

"She looks," Bishop said absently, "like a thoroughbred."

The half-closed bloodshot eye flashed open and Dyal fastened a stare on him. "That surprise you?"

"Some!"

The rancher showed his teeth in a barking laugh. "You're damn blunt! So'm I. I'll pay five thousand for her safe return here—when and if she's returned!"

"Then it's a deal."

"Wait a minute!" Dyal stuck out a thick forefinger. "If she's not returned in ten days I'll throw everything I've got into hunting down those who took her!"

"Ten days isn't long," Bishop said. "It's a cold trail, a month old. She could be a thousand miles away."

"You know better! I've paid out two ransoms, two weeks apart. One was picked up in San Antonio, the other thirty miles out near Calaveras. She's somewhere around that country."

"That's only a guess. You haven't searched."

"They threatened to kill her if I did. So I held off. But after all this time—"

"If you'd got in touch with me right away," Sutter broke in irritably, "you might have had her back and saved your money!"

"Might!" Frank Wittrock said. "Mr. Dyal couldn't gamble with the life of his daughter, Sheriff!"

"He gambled ten thousand dollars and didn't get her back!" Sutter retorted. "I hate to say it, but by now I doubt she's alive!"

Or, Bishop thought, wishful to live, perhaps. He said, "Give me a fair crack at finding her. Or finding what happened to her."

"Ten days," Simon Dyal stated. "I'll wait no longer!"

"It's not enough time."

"Ten days!"

Bishop shrugged. "I'd better get started, then. Loan me a horse. Mine's used up."

"Pick one out for yourself," Dyal said. "Be back in ten days with my daughter!"

He was throwing his saddle on the borrowed Hatchet horse when Sutter walked up to him. Sutter said with a jerk of his head toward the house, "He means it! In ten days he'll turn loose every manhunter he can hire!"

"And you?"

"I'll throw in all the law I can raise!"

"On my trail?" Bishop asked him.

"You know it!" Sutter shot back grimly. "You're the only man in a month who's come up with anything like an idea of who took her. You know something about it, don't you?"

"I put a rumor and a guess together," Bishop said, "and it added up to a hunch. That's all."

Sutter shook his head. "D'you think we can believe that? You think Dyal can? No! Our one chance is that your trail will lead to his daughter. If you don't bring her back in ten days we're coming after you!"

"Dyal made that clear." Bishop fitted his bridle on the borrowed horse. "This Hatchet seems a queer outfit. Dyal's a family man and well off, king of the country. But he lives like a tramp in a barn. Where's his wife?"

"Dead," Sutter said. "They separated some years ago. She and the daughter lived in another house—that one yonder." He pointed off to a rooftop distantly visible through the trees. "It's one of the houses Dyal got from buying up his neighbors' ranches. Mrs. Dyal—her name was Anne, beautiful woman—she fixed it over. Made it a nice place, garden and all, and took up painting for something to do."

Bishop thought of the portrait hanging in Dyal's cheerless house. "I guess she had talent."

"She was a real refined lady," Sutter said, his tone indicating that refinement automatically conferred artistic talent. "A fire started one night last summer in her painting room. Oily rags, I guess. Smoke poured through the house. Kerry managed to get up and give the alarm. Dyal's men got there in time to save most of the house, but not her mother. She never woke up. They found her in bed, dead of the smoke."

"Where did Kerry go then?"

"Nothing to do but move back in with Dyal. After all, he was her father. She took it damn hard, her mother's death. I think, in a way, she almost blamed Dyal for it. Mighty unhappy girl."

It offered reason enough, perhaps, Bishop reflected, for Kerry Dyal to have run away of her own free will at the first opportunity. That barren household and that ugly, rough old Texas rawhider who kept gunmen on his payroll. A dreary life for a young girl. A chilling life, if she also blamed her mother's death on her father.

"Why did Dyal's wife leave him?"

"Nobody knows. He gave her everything she wanted. The house was kept up in those days. Finest place in the Hill Country. Dyal was a home-body, proud of her and their fine house, proud of their little daughter. It was only after they left him . . ." Sutter heaved a sigh. "Folks make their own misery."

"Maybe the girl knows why," Bishop murmured half to himself. "Maybe it's better she shouldn't come back."

The county sheriff stared at him. "That," he stated, "could get you killed before you leave Hatchet! By God, you sound in favor of those who took her! Two ransoms paid and she's still not back!"

He remained staring after Bishop as he rode off. "What's your share?" he hollered, but got no reply.

On approaching it, the house looked sound to Bishop, but walking his horse around to the front he saw the burned-out windows and smoke-streaked walls. Anne Dyal's painting room, built on at one end of the house, stood gutted and roof-

20

less. The other end of the house had escaped damage. His horse, when he ground-reined it, showed a sly disposition to investigate a flower bed. He started to lead the horse off, before another glance showed him that the flower garden was overgrown and choked with weeds, no longer worth protecting. He looked into the burned-out painting room. Nothing was to be seen there but charred walls and the remains of the collapsed roof.

"Wasting my time."

The absentminded carelessness of an amateur lady artist engrossed in her work, probably not realizing that a pile of oily and paint-daubed rags made a hazard. Spontaneous combustion. Smoldering for hours, smoking, suddenly bursting into flames in the night. A rapidly spreading fire. A girl scrambling out of the burning house. The lady sleeping peacefully on in her bed, unaware of the sense-deadening, strangling smoke. She never knew what killed her.

Moving on to the undamaged part of the house, he pushed open an unlocked door and looked into a room that might still have been lived in.

Chairs still stood arranged neatly on the rugs. There were pictures, curtains, a tiny desk, a round table covered with a lace cloth. It had been left untouched in the silent desolation, a kind of memorial, he supposed, to Anne Dyal. Left so by Simon Dyal? No, he decided; by Kerry Dyal. She and her mother must have been very close, living together for years, apart from the old man.

He backed out, closing the door behind him, and walked to his horse. Wasted his time. Something, the county sheriff's words or a nagging curiosity, or both, had nudged him to take a look here and learn what he could before he left Hatchet. But there was nothing to find. Or if there was, he had missed it. He'd never had occasion to go poking around a year-old-fire for pointers to a missing girl. Nor anywhere else.

He and the horse weren't yet acquainted comfortably, so when his boot bonged a can lying in the weeds of the flower bed the horse threw up its head, snorting and rolling an eye suspiciously at him.

Bishop said, " 'Scuse me!" and caught the hanging reins. "Only an oil can."

He looked down at it. A coal-oil can with a spout, the kind found at any ranch house. Anne Dyal had probably used it to hold her linseed oil or turpentine. Or something to clean the

21

brushes with. And tossed it out when empty. Another sign of her carelessness.

Two horsemen, Simon Dyal and Owl Osterberg, came riding out of the trees. Simon Dyal flattened a hand backward for Osterberg to pull up, and came on alone. "What the hell you doing here, Bishop?" he shouted.

Bishop waited for the Hatchet owner to come up to him, and asked, "Why? Is it private?" He watched Osterberg pull a rifle from his saddle boot and swiftly check the breech.

"It damn well is!" Dyal's face was dark with anger. His thick lower lip jutted out. "Nobody comes here! Nobody! I don't allow it!"

"Sorry." Bishop kept his eyes on Osterberg's rifle. "Nobody living here. Took fire, I see. Pity. Could be a nice place, a nice home for somebody."

Dyal turned his head and looked at the house. Gradually his high color subsided. He worked his twisted mouth as if trying for words that would explain his anger at Bishop's trespass.

"My wife's house. And my daughter's. Her things are in there yet—my wife's things. She died in the fire, and I . . ." He brought his open eye around to Bishop. "That's why I—I don't let anybody come here." His brief moment of regret passed, and the rough anger flared up again. "Get out of here, Bishop! Get off Hatchet! Go get my daughter!"

"Sure, sure."

"Ten days, mind! Ten days!"

Passing Osterberg, Bishop said to him, "Put away the rifle, Owl, this isn't Piedras Negras!" And Osterberg stared back at him with his big round eyes, saying nothing.

Riding on, he looked back through the trees. Osterberg sat like a statue, immensely patient, waiting for his boss, waiting because of Dyal's law that nobody must trespass upon that forbidden ground. Dyal, at the edge of the neglected flower bed, still gazed at the house. Had he ever entered it since the death of his wife? Did he sometimes visit it alone when bleak memories haunted him? It was difficult to imagine the grim old man in a sentimental mood. But one never could tell. He did look lonely now, and sorrowful.

Then he saw Dyal turn his head and deliberately spit into the flower bed as if to deny any weakness of grief, and the illusion was shattered. It brought back to Bishop's mind the discarded oil can. The thought stayed with him and he mulled it over while heading down the road toward Forks.

Something wrong about that oil can. Anne Dyal might have thrown it out, but not there, not in her own garden. She had kept that flower bed well-tended up until the night of her death. Last summer it must have been in full bloom. No, she wouldn't have committed the the thoughlessly vandal act. Somebody else might have tossed it there, perhaps since the weeds took over. But why? Who? Nobody but Simon Dyal went near the place.

He had a foul vision of the can in stealthy hands, coal oil pouring from the spout. A match scraped a light. Flames. The can flung hastily into the flower bed, and a figure slipping off in the dark.

"I don't like this caper!" he muttered. "Should've headed straight for Mexico. Damn that Karl!"

He decided to avoid Forks. His reception there had not been cordial when he had stopped to inquire directions to Hatchet headquarters. The place was nothing but a few un-painted buildings sprawled around a saloon at the crossroads, and Hatchet was its chief reason for existence. The trade from Hatchet hands supported it. He'd had enough of Hatchet for this day.

No, he'd push on through until he struck the San Antonio road. His horse was up to it. If Dyal's daughter was anywhere within the vicinity of San Antonio, with Don Ricardo de Risa, it shouldn't be too impossible to track her down.

Herr Risa. He grinned briefly. He knew that pistolero, knew him only too well. Could spot him a mile off. Of course, Don Ricardo could spot him just as fast, unfortunately, and was a past master at deadly tricks. But he just might make it in ten days. He just might.

THREE

The adobe streets of San Antonio spread out raggedly like the strands of an untidy web spun by a blind spider. All day the sun blazed down through the clear dry air, emptying the street during afternoon hours when all right-minded people followed the practice of siesta. The day's dwindling brought them forth to breathe the cooling crispness of a dependable breeze. San Antonio was so healthful, they bragged, if a man wanted to die he had to go somewhere else to do it. This didn't throw death out of work. He could always get himself killed.

Bishop paused by the Alamo to get his bearings. Already its pale wall was drowned in purple shadow, while above it the sky curved crystal blue. The hour balanced between afternoon and evening. Having no time to meditate on the fate of Austin and his devoted fire-eaters, he continued his quest.

He was making the rounds of the livery stables, inquiring after a surrey that a month ago might have been rented by a Mexican gentleman who left with one woman and returned with two. So far he had gained nothing except a strong feeling that two men were following him about the town. Thieves, perhaps, marking his good saddle, stalking him in hopes of an unguarded moment. San Antonio's thieves would steal a man's hat off his head. On the other hand, perhaps they were not thieves.

He sighted one of them now seated on the step of a botica, a Latin-dark man smoking a brown cigarette. Bishop touched his horse on around the Alamo and his feeling became a certainty when the man rose languidly and walked after him.

Back of the Alamo, in a narrow street that barely missed being an alley, he found another livery stable, small and makeshift, run by an aging Irishman whose breath was heavy with the sweetish fumes of tequila. Two ancient cronies squatted on kegs in the half-darkness. It looked too rundown and unprosperous to offer a wheelbarrow for rent, but here Bishop struck paydirt.

"A surrey," said the Irishman, "and a Mexican. Aye, me

cousin who ain't in the livery business at all, but him and his wife own a drygoods store, damn their pinching souls, didn't he throw it in me face that he let the loan of it for a fat price? A rich Mexican, mind! Against the laws of nature, it is! I'm a poor man—"

Bishop dug out a gold piece, feeling suddenly generous. "Let's send somebody for a bottle."

"No need to send out," said the Irishman, accepting the gold piece. "If you don't mind tequila." He produced a bottle. "First drink to you."

The bottle was half empty. "I don't mind tequila," Bishop said. He drank and handed the bottle back. "Where's the Mexican now?"

"Caught the night stage down to Laredo, him and his two women, soon's he got back with me cousin's surrey."

"Laredo? You sure?"

"The Laredo stage is the only one leaves at night, and the three of 'em went on it."

Bishop rubbed his jaw. Laredo. A good hundred and fifty miles south, smack on the border where the Rio Grande ran shallow at this time of year and anybody could splash across and vanish into Mexico without a trace. There went his ten-day deadline.

He had brought his horse into the livery stable, and the Irishman, setting his bottle aside, observed that the animal looked in sore need of a rubdown and rest. His two ancient cronies left their roosts to give him a hand. One of them, peering with beady-bright eyes at its brand, exclaimed, "Hatchet! Ain't that Simon Dyal's outfit up in the Hill Country? Big outfit, huh, mister?"

"Big enough," Bishop said shortly. He was thinking of Laredo, recalling what he could of it from one or two brief visits in the past, and running over in his recollection the possible hangouts that Don Ricardo might make use of down that way. Don Ricardo couldn't have taken Kerry Dyal far into Mexico. Too inconvenient to maintain a contact by which to collect ransom from her father.

The two ancients were dredging up reminiscences concerning Simon Dyal, contradicting and correcting each other, as they worked on the horse.

"Was a stock dealer here forty years ago. That's how he got his start."

"Nope! He raised horses out along the river. Did some

25

freighting too, and trading, a bit of everything. Got in trouble with a woman."

"I'm talking about young Simon Dyal who got his start stock dealing. He married some kind of actressy woman. Married her!"

"Ain't that trouble?"

They both cackled. Bishop watched a shadow out front, the shadow of a man standing motionless alongside the open entrance to the shed. He asked the pair, to keep them talking, "Does Dyal ever get down here?"

They shook their heads in agreement on that.

"Not since he moved up to the Hill Country for good. He left here after this actressy woman he married run away. She took their kid and run off to Houston with a drummer."

"New Orleans! He was a newspaper fella. I heard later they died there of yellow fever."

"Houston! They died in a fire!"

"New Orleans, you dribblin' ol' fool!"

The shadow was gone. Bishop stepped to the door and looked along the narrow street. Two horsemen jogged into it but he saw nothing of the man who had followed him. Behind him the Irishman said, "I never met Dyal. A go-getter, they say, with a heart that hard you could strike a light off it! He ships through here sometimes, but there's a fella that keeps his books for him that does his business."

"Wittrock?"

"Some name like that. A fancy Dan, that one, but the Hatchet ducks that come in with him take his orders like gospel."

"He's Dyal's business manager." Bishop turned back into the shed.

"A hell of a big man he must be now, to be paying a business manager! Some git all the luck!"

The two old men still bickered hotly on the subject of Dyal's actressy woman wife and child of long ago, whether they died of New Orleans yellow fever or in a Houston fire. They agreed that the woman had had a flashy kind of name that went with her looks, and that Simon Dyal had been hard put to keep his eye on the wench both before and after marriage, but they couldn't settle on the identity of the man she ran away with. He was a stranger from somewhere.

They were at it, making positive assertions from hazy recollections, when the pair of horsemen drew up before the livery shed.

26

In the manner of their dismounting Bishop caught a warning. They swung down too quickly for casualness, a little too stiff-legged, like men having a definite purpose. He glanced at the Irishman and saw only a faint puzzlement in the faded eyes, as if trade from an unexpected source surprised him. This was the poorest stable in the town and the two men looked able to afford better. They wore boots and Stetsons, but their clothes showed none of the wear of working cowpunchers. Each carried a gun in a holster that was trimmed down to expose fully the hammer and all of the trigger guard.

One of them halted a step inside the doorway. He had the open face and frank eyes of a trusting boy, and a smile played over his lips. The other, a dark man with the intent expression and thrusting manner of a fanatic, advanced in short paces. He stopped by Bishop's horse but didn't look at it. His voice crackled a demand.

"You got a bill of sale for this horse?"

Bishop gazed at him, his face saturnine, betraying nothing of his instant of surprise at the head-on directness of the challenge. His thoughts raced. The two men who had followed him about the town all day, then, were not sneak thieves. Their task had been to keep him in sight, to mark his every move, every word, and at the critical moment to flag in the killers.

This was the moment and this broken-down livery shed was the place. He silently cursed himself for allowing it. A shoot-out in San Antonio was the last thing he wanted. These two were very sure of themselves. Don Ricardo's men? It wasn't like friend Rico to hire professional gunmen to guard his back trail. Not his style. Besides, these men knew the horse was borrowed from Hatchet. No bill of sale. They had been told. He countered the dark man's demand with a demand of his own.

"You got a right to ask?"

The dark man moved his toes a little farther apart. "Yeah!"

"Show it!" Bishop said, and both men showed instantly, their fingers stroking upward with expert precision.

His right hand dipped under his coat and out again in the flicker of a cross-draw and the barrel of his heavy black gun lined up while the dark man's arms still moved. He had a thin hope of blocking off a shooting, and for that fraction of a second he held his fire and let them weigh their chances.

The dark man, nearest to him and directly under the muzzle of the black gun, froze his draw. But it was only to pass the play to his partner. They were a team out to score, not to be thrown off by any display of proficiency.

The man in the doorway took the play readily and completed his draw. Bishop twitched his gun over at him, his regret not slowing his hand. A cold exasperation was all he felt for this pair of overconfident trigger men. His regret was for the consequences to himself, pushed into a gun fight at the wrong time in the wrong town.

His shot shook the man in the doorway. The frank eyes aged and the open face drained gray and pinched. The dark man, not seeing the result of the shot on his partner behind him unflinchingly took his swift turn at the kill. Bishop fired again.

The dark man fell against the Hatchet horse, gasping a complaint, "Goddam! Why wasn't we told he—"

The horse reared and knocked him off sprawling. The Irishman snatched up his precious tequila bottle to save it from breakage, before joining his two ancient cronies who dived squawling into a horse stall.

Bishop dodged the plunging Hatchet horse and headed at once for the street. San Antonio took a stern view of shootings these days within its allegedly law-abiding precincts, and likely enough the two gunmen held rank as special deputies by favor of some local politician. Also, a Texas Ranger or two could usually be counted on to come along and take up where the town law left off.

He shouldered aside the man in the doorway, who was trying to lift his gun as if it weighed eighty pounds, and caught up the reins of the nearest of the two horses. Faces peered from the little adobe houses, but the street showed empty. He swung onto the horse and heeled it to a run.

A man wearing a badge pinned to his shirt loomed up before him in the gathering dust, hastily loading a shotgun. Bishop's gun came out and his voice rasped, "Drop it!"

The man dropped it and jumped back, to dart forward and retrieve it after Bishop clattered past. "Halt!" he yelled.

At the first cross street Bishop leaned to wheel his horse and cleared the corner a shade ahead of the shotgun's blast. The charge of whistling pellets struck adobe with a sound like stones on a muffled drum. He cut on through to another straggling street and wheeled again, his course southward. He guessed with any luck he could get out of San Antonio without too much further trouble. The law would take awhile

28

to size up what had happened and build up a big search for him. Not long, but enough to give him a head start.

Night was coming on. He reined the horse to a more sedate gait, trusting to avoid attention, until the fringe of town thinned out, and became scattered dots of tiny ranchitos and humble jacales. There'd be a pursuit, no question of that. How far and how long it might last was another matter. Ahead lay a vast stretch of brush and prickly pear where outlaw cattle ate huijillo beans and Spanish dagger. Hungry country, mostly dry, but a man with eyes in his head could dodge the posses there until they tired of the game and went home.

Somewhere far down there he'd change horses. Or turn loose this one and catch a southbound stage to Laredo. Risky trip. Have to keep his eyes open, sleep on the fly, watch out for Rangers and signs of Don Ricardo de Risa.

Watch out for signs of Hatchet too, he mused. Someone had hired the two gunmen to cut him down. Someone who knew him only slightly, else they would have got forewarning to shoot on sight and take no chances. That ruled out the Don, who knew him well. It let in Simon Dyal, a stay-at-home who knew the name of Rogue Bishop only as that of a man who had sided against some friends of his up in Cedar Valley.

Simon Dyal, bitter old range shark whose payroll supported gun hands. Whose estranged wife died in a fire that probably was set by somebody with a can of coal oil. Whose daughter had gone missing a month past, no word to the law. There was only Simon Dyal's word for it that he had paid out two ransoms. His word wasn't worth much, if he had already broken the ten-day deadline by sending gunmen after the man who was trying to trace his daughter. Maybe he didn't want her back. Maybe he had even arranged her abduction, only hell knew why.

In that case, no reward this trip, and the risks running high from all directions.

Bishop fished out a cigar and bit into it. "Well," he muttered, "I was headed for Mexico anyway. . . ."

The philosophical thought failed to lift him into a detached mood. In his mind's eye he saw the portrait of Kerry Dyal. The brooding eyes. The haunting air of puzzled loss, almost of tragedy. A girl like that, young, strikingly attractive, should have gay laughter, warmth, a joyous and outgoing eagerness. That was her due and she had been cheated of it.

If the painting truly portrayed her, she was a lonely and unhappy girl, withdrawn and on the defensive.

She could have changed since then, of course. Especially this past month. Probably held captive in some border hideout in or near Laredo. No knowing what she'd be like a few months hence. If she lived.

He guessed he just might go on searching for her. He just might do that.

FOUR

Laredo didn't altogether match Bishop's limited recollections of it. An alien air of bustling disturbed the old easygoing atmosphere. The narrow streets looked familiar with their low thatch-roofed houses of stone and sun-dried adobe bricks, but some new buildings were going up here and there, buildings that boasted high false fronts and tall windows.

Americans—norteamericanos—had always been a very small minority here and made slight impact on the Mexican inhabitants. Now an increase of the Americans could be noticed. They moved briskly as if short of time, talked of facts and figures, were impatient of elaborate courtesies, and their eyes looked for tomorrow.

The railroad was pushing steadily west to Laredo, from Corpus Christi on the Gulf of Mexico, bringing with it the promise of trade and new markets. A boom was rising. Despite its clinging regard for the past, Laredo was having to prepare for the future.

Even Laredo. It was actually organizing a mixed American-Mexican police force. Policemen—in Laredo! The old dons and doñas shook their heads. *Que lástima!* What next? Certain others wrung their hands. The coming of the railroad might put an end to the hoary and honored trade of smuggling. *Ay de mi!*

With his fingers Bishop massaged the cramped muscles at the back of his neck. He had used up five days getting here, the last two days and night in a crowded stagecoach that he flagged down and squeezed aboard after abandoning his horse.

The pursuit out of San Antonio had proved stubborn, not so much on the part of the posse, which quit the second morning, as by five riders whose interest in the matter kept him ducking through the chaparral until anger disposed him to stand and make a brush-fight of it. Persistent, those five. They weren't Texas Rangers. One of them he thought was Jay Nunn of the Hatchet spread.

Later they flashed past the lumbering stagecoach, riding

in the same direction, wearing bandannas tied up to their eyes against the dust. The leather side-curtains of the coach were closed for the same reason. They had picked up his abandoned horse and evidently had thought he had got hold of a fresh mount somewhere, for they swept by and went racing on.

The odds had it that they had come all the way and got here a day ahead of him. They could still be scouring the town, but he figured it likely that they had finished that job and then bedded down to catch some sleep. They had kept hard on the go since leaving San Antonio, practically every hour in the saddle, wearing out horses and themselves. The stagecoach, though it was no cushioned carriage, had allowed him to doze and rest for two days.

He needed to hole up somewhere for a while. A hotel wouldn't do. Too much risk of running into them, of another gunfight in another strict town. Give them time to quit and pull out, then do some town-scouring of his own. Needed a horse and saddle too. Attend to that later.

Keeping sharp watch and staying off main streets, he made his way to the riverfront. Here everything remained the same as ever, undisturbed by any American touch, as Mexican as the little Mexican town of Nuevo Laredo across the river. Shacks perched along the high riverbank, each having its scrap of garden fenced to guard it from the loose goats and burros. The air was tangy with the odor of chili and frijoles, and any man could locate an unmarked cantina by following his nose along the fragrant path of ginebra, aguardiente, tequila, and wine.

Bishop bent his head under the doorway of a low-ceilinged cantina and entered. He bent it again to the dark gaze of two thin men and a plump woman who sat listening to a youth softly strumming a homemade guitar. The youth stopped playing and placed his hand flat on the strings.

In the most florid Spanish at his command Bishop said, "Pray continue. I return from too long in the Texas wilds, and your music is sweet to my ears! If we may drink also, the greater pleasure to me."

They smiled, dark eyes softening. An Americano, this big hard-visaged man. A pistolero, said the twin bulges under his black coat. But a man of understanding and discrimination. Simpatico. One of their kind. The plump woman rose, took orders all around, and ceremoniously filled them. The two

32

men and the youth saluted Bishop with raised glasses. The woman remained standing, as did Bishop.

"Señor, be seated."

"Señora, I wait for you."

The youth returned to his guitar playing. Bishop placed money on the skimpy bar. It was pleasant to sit here sipping tequila and listening to the quiet strumming, but it wasn't getting him anywhere. The courtesies having been observed, he mentioned he was looking for a posada or any modest lodging where privacy was valued.

They understood immediately. Privacy at times was of first importance. Nothing could give her greater happiness, said the plump woman, than to be able to oblige him. But it was not to be found along the riverfront. Not since Laredo had got itself a police force. Many of the police were Mexicans, *por dios,* of low class. Spies and snoopers, for money they would betray anybody.

However, there was a place farther back from the river, yet not too close in town, run by a woman of discretion, Dee Hazard. She was not Mexican, and her discretion unfortunately was based on the amount of money involved, but several people had found privacy and security in her place. It had no name. The youth would go with Bishop and point it out to him.

Bishop paid for another round of drinks and left with the youth. He hadn't much faith that the place would fill his requirements. The Mexican idea of privacy was often pretty broad, and if the new police of Laredo were prying into this quarter, as the plump woman had intimated . . .

"There, Señor!" the youth said, pointing. "The place that has the red door and the two large windows."

Except for the red door, the building appeared to be an ordinary American saloon that had fallen on bad times. The dirt of years dimmed the two front windows. The wooden front step was broken, and curled old bits of dried paint hung on the walls like chicken feathers.

Bishop had a mind to pass up the place. The plump woman had meant well, but he could do better than this sorry dive. He raised his eyes idly to the board above the windows before remembering that the place had no name. The board had once flaunted a name and it had been painted over, but so thinly that the lettering ghosted through: WITTROCK'S SQUARE DEAL BAR.

The name rang a bell. Wittrock. Frank Wittrock, Simon

33

Dyal's business manager. Obviously the name of a former owner. Not too surprising if the owner had been Frank Wittrock. Nothing against a smart young man acquiring a saloon in the course of his career. Nor was it odd that the saloon should be in Laredo. Many young men of the South came by this route, bound for California or wherever they thought fortune was beckoning them.

The broken step creaked dismally under his weight. The red door didn't give to his touch. A woman's voice inside called, "Push, stranger!"

Stranger? Her regulars knew about the sticking door. He didn't, so she knew he must be a stranger. Maybe it was purposely fixed that way. He thrust the door open and stepped inside.

The interior was about as he had expected. A chipped bar, the streak-smeared top decorated with burns and rings. Fly-specked mirrors, cloudy glasses. A poker table, its green cloth worn to holes, four chairs shoved askew as the last players had left them. A one-time prosperity was hinted at by a sign tacked above the dusty back-bar shelves: ONLY BEST KENTUCKY WHISKEY SERVED HERE.

"Got to fix that door someday," the woman said, going behind the bar. She had the nasal voice of bad temper and a sharp face to go with it, under a pile of hair too brightly yellow to be true. "What'll it be?"

"Whiskey."

She set out a bottle and glass. He poured, tasted the whiskey, and glanced up at the sign. "The best is none too good, Miss Hazard!"

"How'd you know my name?"

"I was looking for privacy and got steered here. What's the Dee stand for?"

"Delight."

Hell's delight, he thought, the names they do pick. "The man I spoke to," he said, "was named Wittrock."

Her guarded manner underwent a change. She leaned white elbows on the bar. "Frank? Where'd you see him?"

"North." He emptied his glass. A second drink helped take the curse off the first. "He was in cattle, sort of."

She straightened up, shaking her head. "Not Frank! That son-of-a-bitch doesn't know cattle! Cards, fast talk, juggling figures, any kind of flimflam—but not cattle!"

Bishop shrugged. "Light eyes, pale hair, pale skin. Not as young as he might seem to be. Talks like a Southerner—"

"That's Frank, sure! If I could get my hands on—" She lowered her voice. "He a friend of yours?"

"No. When did he own this place?"

"We owned it together. He came to Texas with money he took from a bank he worked for. He had some left when I met him, and I had some." Her greenish-blue eyes narrowed. "Did he turn his big trick, do you know?"

"Which trick was that?"

"The one he went up to San Antonio about. He came back and said he was onto a big one, real big. Then he packed his things and went off again, and I haven't seen him since." She struck the bar with her hand. "Took every cent and left me the bills to pay! Three years ago. Three years I've been trying to dig out from under. This was a nice place. You wouldn't believe what a nice business we had here."

"I bet I wouldn't," Bishop said.

She went on unheeding, "Oh, Frank was always pulling his flimflams, sure, but they mostly worked okay. He was sharp, I'll say that. And close-mouthed. Never told me his right name. It was Trevor something."

"Never knew a Trevor," Bishop remarked. "Good name to leave behind, I guess." He would have thought Beauregard, something on that order, more fitting to that pale young-old Southerner.

"He had a gold watch and it was engraved inside the case. 'To Trevor from Mother with love.' Hah! From Mother with love! Him!" Delight Hazard reached behind her for a tumbler, poured herself a stiff three fingers from the bottle and tossed it off. "Once in a while his flimflams didn't pay off and it looked bad for him, but he had friends to help him out. Not friends, exactly. Connections he called them. He knew every snake-eyed dodger for miles around. Some of them still come in here."

"D'you happen to know one who calls himself de Risa?" Bishop asked. "Don Ricardo de Risa?"

Warily the greenish-blue eyes blanked over. "Naw!"

Too prompt, her denial. He took two gold pieces from his pocket, twenties. He lay one on the bar and held the other in his hand. "My name's Bishop."

"Heard of you." She looked up quickly from the coins to his face and back again.

"And de Risa?"

Greed struggled briefly with caution, and won. "I've heard his name spoken. Some tough Mexicans come in here at times. Polite but tough. Y'know the kind. I don't talk their lingo but I know what they're saying. I think they ride for him."

"Would I find him in Nuevo?"

She shook her head. "No, he's up the river. About a day's ride, from what they said. Or he was, then. Last they were in here was three weeks, maybe a month ago. That's the best I can do."

"It'll do." Bishop placed the second twenty with the first and turned to leave.

"Wait," she said. "You came here for privacy. I've got it. A room at the back, under the floor. Five dollars a day."

"Later, maybe." He had no intention of burying himself alive. "I've got to see about getting a horse."

"If you're crossing the river tonight you won't need a horse," she called after him. "Some fellas are running a ferry at the foot of the Calle."

He looked back. The two coins had disappeared. "Thanks. Hope trade picks up."

She nodded, striking a match to light the lamps. Darkness was coming fast. "I think my luck's turning!"

He spent the better part of two hours finding a horse he wanted and then a saddle that suited him, haggling over the price because his money was running low. The horse was a dun that looked to have speed and endurance, and although it was inclined to be cold-jawed on first acquaintance, he expected they'd get along after awhile. He walked it a roundabout route to the dark riverfront, and on the high bank he looked up along the river toward the foot of the Calle for a glimpse of the ferry that Delight Hazard had said was running. There was no sign of it, no light, though he waited a long time. He frowned, thinking he should have asked her if it ran at night and if it accommodated a horse.

"Señor!"

It was the lad from the cantina, breathless, gliding up beside him, the whites of his eyes glistening in the dark. The dun horse shivered.

"What is it?" Bishop murmured.

"Señor, I search for you everywhere! Do not go to the ferry! Five men come here asking for you. We know nothing. They go to the place of the Hazard woman. They greet her as one greets a friend. Soon they come out and go quickly down to the ferry. They are waiting there now!"

"Damn!" Bishop muttered, but felt no particular animosity toward Delight Hazard for betraying him. One always took that chance, dealing with her kind. She had sold him out, no doubt, for a price. This was her lucky day and she was making the most of it.

He said to the lad, "I must cross the river tonight."

"Si, Señor! There is a ford. The old smuggler's ford close by Fort McIntosh up the river. The fort is now empty. One can cross there if careful. Does your horse fear water?"

"I'll find out." Bishop parted with another twenty, pressing it into the lad's hand. *"Gracias!"*

He had to thread a crooked course through town, avoiding lights, then back to the river where he found a path along the bank. As he rode, he considered what Delight Hazard had told him of Don Ricardo de Risa. If true—and she'd had no reason to lie to him at that moment—the Don was camped somewhere in the vicinity of Lago Blanco. Or he had been, up to a few weeks ago. A permanent camp not too far from the border, convenient for raiding into Texas for cattle and horses, one of the Don's common occupations when nothing better offered itself.

The walls of Fort McIntosh loomed up blackly, and he drew in to listen. The only sound was the soft gurgle of water. He nudged the dun on, veering left, feeling the bank shelve downward until the dun's forefeet sank into wet sand. The river widened here, running shallow, the far bank bulking low against the night sky. Before him stretched a gravel bar, a thin island separated from the bank, and he murmured to the dun, "Let's have your opinion of water!"

To the touch of his heels, the horse explored forward. Water rose to its chest, receded, and it lunged onto the gravel bar and paced on, dipping its head to the compliment of Bishop's slap on the neck.

"You'll do!"

He thought he heard a whistle. He brought the horse to a standstill, listening, but water lapping against the gravel bar raised a barrier of sound. Nor could he decide where the whistle had come from, behind or ahead. He caught a small noise and peered back. The blackness could have hidden anything, a man or an army.

The noise, a quiet thumping, ceased. He knew then that a horse had come down the bank and halted at the river's edge. If it had a rider, the man was either waiting for others to join him before advancing farther, or was spying out over the

37

river for sight of a moving target. The whistle meant that there was more than one. Border patrol, perhaps. Rangers looking for smugglers. Or the trackers—the persistent five. Possibly more than five by now.

Bishop drew a gun. He had to find out. Couldn't wait here on the gravel bar making no sound, like a treed bobcat for the hunters to bring down. He snapped the hammer back, hard, letting the snick of it be heard, and instantly a rifle shot spanged, answering the question. He fired twice at the flash.

In the midst of a floundering splash a man's voice wailed, "Goddam it, come on! He's—"

The dun's hoofs rattled the gravel, to the outer edge of the bar where it plunged into the river up to its shoulders, drenching Bishop. Rifles opened up on the Texas side, then abruptly stopped. He heard horses pound down the bank without halt for the man he had spilled.

The river shallowed beyond the channel, and presently the dun trod bottom. It came out of the river with him onto the shoreline below the bank. He swung down, letting it shake itself like a wet dog, and tested both of his guns for dampness. He tested them on the riders, dim figures racing out along the gravel bar. The shells exploded one after another. The riders sprayed out and quit the gravel bar for the river.

He reloaded, mounted the dun, and took off up the shoreline. The firing was going to bring the Alcalde from Nuevo Laredo and all the cohorts he could muster. With luck, they'd be there to confront the hunters, to demand explanations and delay them.

And the law on the Texas side would also be looking into the shooting. That new police force. Bishop shook his head. Progress was all very well. New days, new ways. But not when carried to extremes. The sound old ways, steadfast and durable, should not be lightly sloughed off. He hoped he'd seen the last of Texas, Kerry Dyal regardless. A man could do just so much for a woman, and Texas was too much for him.

FIVE

On its bare hill, the adobe walls of the abandoned Mission of San Silvano shone under the high sun like the walls of a splendid pink-chalk palace. A closer look showed them to be crumbling, long fallen into disrepair.

Below the hill squatted the tiny village of San Silvano, and in the distance shimmered the undrinkable alkali water of Lago Blanco. It made a fair and pretty scene, a peaceful scene—except for three or four big-hatted heads raised above the broken remains of the wall surrounding the mission. Beneath the heads poked the short barrels of carbines.

One of the big hats came off, its owner waving it in a wide circle as a warning signal to Bishop to ride clear. A considerate gesture, offering to him the option of minding his own business or getting shot. Bishop returned the wave and stayed on course. The carbines leveled, waiting for him to come within range.

Another head raised, hands holding field glasses trained on him. He heard on the still air a voice rap a command, and he breathed freer. A slim figure sprang up and beckoned him on.

Bishop grinned unkindly. Don Ricardo wouldn't have him shot down before satisfying his curiosity as to the purpose of this unexpected visit. Trust him for that. Trust him for little else.

The Don paid him the courtesy of coming out to meet him on foot. He was dapper and graceful, dressed in full charro garb: frogged jacket, tight pants, pleated shirt, his boots stitched as ornamentally as his gun belts. Hardworn finery, showing some frazzle, result of living the life of an *hombre del campo*, but elegant. Always elegant. His elaborately embroidered sombrero he carried in his hand, his right hand, to signify peace. An empty formality, that, as he could exchange the hat for a gun in a flash. And anyway his left hand was as fast as his right.

"Rogue—*compadre!*"

They met. Bishop dismounted. "Hi, Rico!"

They did not shake hands.

Later, in the mission yard, Bishop counted nine men. Not nearly so many as Rico usually had with him. The Don had once commanded a rebel army of thousands and formed the habit of thinking in large numbers. A *muy grande caballero*, keen, intelligent, highly dangerous. His slightly blunted features saved him from too much handsomeness, while his debonair quality lent him a wholly deceptive youthfulness.

"How's the cattle market these days, Rico?"

Don Ricardo shrugged one shoulder. They sat in the shade of the chapel building, smoking, drinking a good dry wine that Bishop fancied had come from far away. "As usual, Rogue." He spoke English with scarcely any accent. "It is a living."

"I don't see any sign of fresh cattle around here."

"No. I obtain orders from the buyers and fill them direct from the—er—from the source. No holdover."

Bishop nodded, accepting the glib explanation without believing it. The Don's men looked prosperous. They wore expensive boots that showed no signs of hard usage. Four of them were gambling at monte on a spread blanket for fairly stiff stakes. A bad guesser lost a stack of American dollars and quit the game, saying there was more where that came from, and sending a grin at Don Ricardo.

"And how has life been treating you, Rogue?"

"Life's all right. It's Texas that's gone to hell."

Don Ricardo flashed white teeth. "How true! Suddenly they don't care for our kind. I never cross the river for pleasure. Only for business."

Bishop rose, stretching his long arms. "I guess things have been pretty slack with you the past month or so," he remarked. "Or are you resting up from a long trip?"

Through a break in the wall he had a view of the tiny village below. A boy was stoning three goats out of a corn patch. A man shouted at him to stop abusing his goats. Another man took up for the boy and a violent argument ensued. Two women came out of a house to observe the ruckus. One, a matron wearing a dark shawl, let loose a voluble scolding at the two men. The other, apparently much younger, kept silent and turned back to the house. Her step was light and firm, but she did not have the quick flying movements of a young Mexican girl. Bishop switched his gaze to Don Ricardo, who had risen after him.

40

The Don, his dark eyes cool, asked softly, "What brings you here, Rogue Bishop?" The nine men, instantly sensing a rift, ceased all movement.

For answer, Bishop said, "Collecting two ransoms is pushing your luck—Herr Risa!"

The Don thinned his lips, ran a glance over the watching men, then laughed shortly. "Rogue, you amaze me! So you tracked me all the way down here—for what? Knowing you as I do, I'm certain you expect to profit from it, but damned if I know how! Is it Hatchet money?"

Bishop nodded. "Five thousand dollars for the return of the girl!"

Don Ricardo burst out laughing. His laughter was genuine. It bent him over, hands clasping his flat stomach, his shoulders shaking. "Rogue, you've been fooled!" He straightened up, wiping his eyes. "Oh, this is rich! Five thousand dollars for—" Laughter choked him again. "Rogue Bishop to the rescue! *Compadre*, it does me good to see you made a fool of!"

Bishop glared at him. "What are you trying to tell me?"

"Let the young lady tell you!" Don Ricardo chuckled. "Go down and talk to her!"

"I'm about to do that!"

"Do, by all mans," Don Ricardo urged him cheerfully. "On foot, please. We don't want any kidnaping around here!"

Bishop sent him a final glare and stalked down to the village, followed by renewed chuckles from Don Ricardo and the grins of his men.

He was perplexed and in a ruffled mood. Whatever the weird setup here, Rico was supremely sure of himself. He stopped at the house where he had seen the girl enter, and tapped on the open door.

The older woman confronted him, stony-faced. He took off his hat and inclined his head, smothering his prickly humor.

"Señora, a thousand pardons for this intrusion! *Por favor*, allow me to present my respects to Señorita Dyal. I come as a friend—"

"From where?"

The question came from the girl. She stepped forward, and the older woman moved aside. "You come from where?"

"From your home, Hatchet," he said, and she shrank back and he saw fear leap to her eyes.

"Hatchet isn't my home! I have no home! Nobody can take me back there!"

Her vehemence made him blink. The woman moved protectingly closer to her and eyed him with dark distrust.

"Miss Dyal, I came here to—"

"I'll never go back! Never!"

Her portrait had done her justice, no more. She could, he supposed, be called strikingly beautiful but for the unsmiling mouth and the tense expression of guardfulness. Somewhat at a loss, he said, "I thought I was tracking you down for your good. It wasn't too easy."

"Nobody asked you!"

He countered with a half-truth. "As a matter of fact, your father did. He engaged me to find you and take you home." The disbelief on her face stopped him. He shrugged. "Well, that's out! But don't you think you might tell me your side of it, after all my trouble?"

His tone of voice, which he made as gentle as he could, must have allayed some of her fear. She scanned his face searchingly. There was nothing much he could do about his face, but she evidently saw something beyond the hard mouth and predatory beak, for she stepped back and motioned for him to be seated. The woman withdrew to an inner room, leaving the door open. Bishop waited until Kerry Dyal sat down. He pulled up a chair and sat facing her.

"You don't believe your father wants you back?"

She gazed past him at the sunshine in the open doorway, not responding. A moment passed and abruptly she began to talk.

"I found a diary belonging to my mother," she said, "in her desk. After she died. She died in a fire. I had no proof, nothing to go on, but I felt that somebody set fire to the house. My mother was very careful about such things, and taught me to be careful. It couldn't have been an accident. It just couldn't!"

Thinking of the coal-oil can in the garden, Bishop privately was inclined to agree with her.

"In my mother's diary," she went on, "I learned why she and my father lived apart. My father was married before, when he was young. His wife ran off with another man and took their son. Sometime later my father received a newspaper clipping from New Orleans. It was a list of victims of a yellow fever epidemic there. In the list were the names of his wife and son and the man she ran away with."

"So he married again," Bishop said. Some men needed more than one lesson.

"Later, yes. He and my mother were happy. So was I. Then

everything changed. In her diary my mother wrote why. My father got a letter—from his son. His son was a grown man by then. He wrote that he and his mother were still alive. The man she had run off with was a newspaperman who'd been afraid that my father would hunt them down some day, so he had that list printed and sent to him. My father had unknowingly committed bigamy. My mother wasn't really his wife at all! And I—I'm illegitimate!" She buried her face in her hands.

Bishop made to pat her shoulder, but let his hand fall. No use trying to comfort people who placed such store in matters of strict legality. Her mother—that real refined lady—had no doubt considered herself soul-soiled, maybe damned to a Puritan hell for a perfectly innocent mistake. So did her daughter.

Poor little b . . . "Mistakes will happen," Bishop said, and she uncovered her face to send him a withering look for making such a prodigal understatement.

"My mother immediately moved out of my father's house, of course, and I went with her." Kerry Dyal's tone indicated that no other alternative was possible, nor thinkable.

"So I was told." He had to shake off a feeling of depravity for thinking as he did.

"After the fire and my mother's death, there was nothing else for me to do but move back into my father's house. My father was—he had become grim. Hard! We hardly ever exchanged a word."

A sense of guilt on the old man's side, he mused, and on hers the wretched shame of her birth. Made them both self-conscious, unapproachable.

"Then a letter came for me. From his son—my half-brother. My father didn't see it. It was given to me by Frank Wittrock, his business manager."

"Where did he get it?" Bishop asked.

She made an impatient gesture. "One of Frank's duties is to pick up the mail for Hatchet. In his letter, my half-brother warned me that I was in terrible danger. He said my father had actually forced his first wife to run away in fear for her life. My mother, he said, was murdered! The fire wasn't an accident—it was set by my father! And I would be murdered next!"

"How'd he know so much about Hatchet doings?"

"He had a friend there, he said, who wrote and kept him informed. He didn't name him, but I think it was Frank Wittrock. Frank was very understanding and sympathetic. He couldn't openly go against my father, because of his job, but he always found a reason to be close at hand whenever my father and I were together. Anyway, my half-brother wrote that he had made all arrangements for me to escape from Hatchet."

"And that's where de Risa came in."

"Yes. Mr. de Risa made it look as if I had been kidnaped by a gang. He took me to——"

"I know the rest," Bishop interrupted. "But where's this half-brother of yours?"

"He was to have met me here, but he left a note saying that his business had called him unexpectedly to Havana. He's in some kind of import trade, and has to travel a lot."

"What's his name?"

"Trevor Dyal."

Bishop drew out a cigar and eyed it stonily. "Well!" he muttered, and tucked it back. "Well!" A shadow fell across the floor, and he turned his head.

Don Ricardo lounged in the doorway, smiling. "My friend does not bother you too much, I trust, Miss Dyal?" he inquired.

Kerry Dyal shook her head. "Not as long as he doesn't try to take me back to my father! I'm happier here than I've been in a long time. At least," she amended, "I'm not unhappy here."

"Your happiness is my first consideration," Don Ricardo assured her gallantly, smoothing his thin line of mustache with his thumb. "If I could hear the golden sound of your laughter——"

"I forget how it sounds myself."

Bishop stood up and looked at the girl. Incredible, her belief in a letter supposedly written by an alleged half-brother she had never seen. Trusting herself to a stranger, Don Ricardo of all men—it boggled Bishop's imagination to see Rico as a girl's guardian angel. She was a gullible innocent.

And yet—yes, she'd been ripe for the trap. Anything was better than Hatchet, that barren house, the grim old man. The hideous suspicion that her mother was murdered. The fear.

The letter had supplied the final push, and offered escape. At the end of her rope, she had taken the chance.

He left the house with Don Ricardo, and walking up the

hill he said, "The joke's on me! What's the straight of it about this half-brother of hers?"

"Damned if I know," Don Ricardo confessed lightly. "Now that you see the joke, I'll tell you my part in the comedy. A man named Osterberg got in touch with me—"

"Owl Osterberg? Dyal's range boss?"

"The same one who used to head a gang of shooters when the range was open to takers. Before the law slammed down." Don Ricardo sighed for the good old days. "Osterberg offered me a very queer proposition. Simon Dyal wanted rid of his daughter. Devil knows why. The arrangement was that she would be persuaded to meet me, and leave freely with me. But I should make it appear that she was kidnaped, and leave a warning note behind. Did you ever know of anything like it?"

Bishop shook his head. "You were hard up, to take that on!"

"Osterberg would have found somebody else. Some degraded ruffian without my scruples!"

"What scruples?"

Don Ricardo snorted. "Scruples against murdering a young girl—especially a pretty one! Osterberg's instructions from Dyal were that I should send a demand for ransom—five thousand dollars. My pay. I was to do away with her. Leave her body where it would be found, outside San Antonio where I would pick up the ransom. A vicious plot, yes?"

"Vicious is right," Bishop agreed. "And no suspicion on Hatchet. Kidnap gang collects the ransom and kills the girl to keep her from identifying them. H'm! Osterberg wasn't paying you any compliment, picking you for the job!"

"A fortunate error," Don Ricardo said tranquilly. "The girl lives, and I prosper! She is not wanted back on Hatchet, certainly not alive, so I have the whip-hand. Dyal has paid twice. The second payment was picked up near Calaveras. I have not yet decided," he murmured thoughtfully, "where the next one will be!"

"There won't be a next one," Bishop told him. "Dyal swore to me he wouldn't pay another dollar till his daughter's back alive and safe."

"Back alive and safe!" Don Ricardo scoffed. "He wants her dead!"

"Maybe not. That business manager of his, Frank Wittrock —I dug up a thing or two about him. He's on the make. In two days Dyal and the county sheriff will throw everything into a hunt for you."

"So?" Don Ricardo raised a skeptical eyebrow. "I've been hunted before. They wouldn't find me in months!"

"Took me eight days, tangling with Hatchet-hired guns clear down to Laredo."

"Laredo?" The Don frowned. "That is too close! I shall have to shift camp tomorrow and find another place for the girl!"

"Rico," Bishop said, "you're pushing your luck way too far! Let me take her home and have a talk with the county sheriff."

"You joke, Rogue! She is better than a gold mine! Besides, she wouldn't go with you. Only with me. She trusts me."

"Bad judgment! You're the ruin of many a woman."

Don Ricardo grinned. "True, I often find my thoughts fondly lingering on her," he admitted candidly, "but it is to my interest to keep her trust. When are you leaving?"

"I'll let you know."

"No hurry, of course."

" 'Course not."

"As long as you leave before I shift camp tomorrow!"

SIX

They slept on straw in the chapel, a comfort Bishop didn't entirely appreciate, as the rustle of it whenever he moved brought eyes staring solemnly at him in the darkness. Don Ricardo's men mistrusted him, which he allowed they had every right to, they knowing perfectly well his reason for coming here.

They didn't maintain any regular night watch. Occasionally one would rise and lounge out, yawning, carbine dangling, and return shortly. He slept, woke again, and lay gazing up at the stars visible through the broken roof of the chapel. His thoughts bent to the problem of Kerry Dyal. If Rico was right, Simon Dyal had paid out the money to buy his daughter's death. He'd paid twice, by which Rico concluded that the old man would go on paying to stop her from showing up alive.

Yet Dyal had sounded convincingly positive when he declared that he would pay no more until his daughter was delivered to him. He had called in the county sheriff. He had set a ten-day deadline for her return, then broken it by sending gunmen to hunt the hunter. Or somebody had broken it.

In any case, whether Dyal kept on paying or launched a massive hunt, the outcome for Kerry Dyal was bleakly uncertain. She didn't know Rico, didn't realize she was a captive in an outlaw camp, a lamb in the care of a lobo. No future in it. On the other hand, Hatchet also offered black prospects.

Restless, he tugged on his boots and went outside. The tiny village was a dark cluster below the hill. He scowled down at it, his restlessness increasing. He was letting himself get too concerned in the fate of that fool girl. Something about her was stirring an urge in him to snatch her out of Rico's hands. A thankless task, and no definite plan where to take her if he managed it. In the morning Rico and his men would escort her to another hidden camp somewhere, wiping out their tracks. *Adios,* Rogue Bishop—don't try to follow us!

They had stabled his horse with their own in the roofless remains of one of the mission buildings. Quietly, he entered the stable and took down his saddle. The men slept soundly this late in the night, but the chance of getting away unheard was slight. They were alert as wild animals.

He was not surprised when a voice murmured, "You leave, Señor?" Three of the Don's men regarded him, carbines leveled. They were barefooted and had slipped silently to the broken doorway.

"I leave," he said saddling the dun. They were narrowly watching his hands, watching for a glint of metal in the darkness.

"Don Ricardo—"

"My compliments to Don Ricardo. When he wakes up tell him I left while the night was cool."

"At once."

"Let him sleep."

"No, Señor." One of them slipped out of the stable. The remaining two stood motionless, blocking the doorway.

Fitting the bridle on the dun, Bishop asked, "Don't figure to stop me, do you?" His eyes glimmered at them.

One of them sighed. The other said woodenly, "It is for Don Ricardo—"

The man who had left uttered a warning yell. His carbine went off. A gun answered it, and he yelled again, painedly. The two men whirled and dashed out, Bishop behind them. The man who had fired his carbine lay in the yard. Don Ricardo came running from the chapel with the rest of his men. He looked down at the fallen man, then at Bishop.

"What the devil are you doing?"

They both had their guns out ready, and glared at each other.

Bishop rasped, "Snub it off! Somebody else shot your man —somebody he fired at!"

Two voices rose in agreement. The Don snapped, "Quiet! Listen!" The beat of a running horse faded into the night.

"A spy, Rico," Bishop murmured. "Left his horse and prowled here on foot!"

The Don swore. "Somebody who tracked you here, no doubt! You bring me bad luck!" He snapped a command to his men, "Make ready to move camp!"

"Change it to saddle and scoot, Rico!" Bishop said. "That joker will soon come back with friends! I'll go pick up the girl."

"No, you won't! Saddle your horse, but stay away from the girl!"

48

"His horse is saddled," a man mentioned.

"It is?" Don Ricardo wagged his head half-admiringly. "Up to one of your tricks, eh? And the spy is part of the trick? I should have guessed it!"

"You guess wrong," Bishop said. "If you're smart you'll move out of here fast!"

"Don't try to stampede me, Rogue. You and I have scraped through many a rough spot together. We understand each other. Ordinarily I enjoy crossing wits with you. But not this time! Stay out of my game!"

"And if I don't?"

Don Ricardo spread his hands eloquently and sauntered back to the chapel.

Bishop stared meditatively after him. Although they had locked horns at times when their purposes happened to collide, and tricked each other shamelessly, never had they so quickly and openly clashed in blunt challenge. Rico had hell in his neck this trip. Growing flinty with the hard-lived years, perhaps. Losing his touch for subtle tactics. Trigger arrogant.

Well, if it had come to that . . .

The Don's scorn of urgency communicated itself to his men. They had acquired some belongings during the weeks of prosperity and ease. Blankets, extra clothes and gear, food supplies, jugs and bottles. Odds and ends of luxury. They had pack horses, and by the light of lanterns they loaded the animals in the yard. They saddled up their mounts. They argued over the man who had got shot, whether to bury him there and then or carry him along for burial elsewhere. Some of them, inclined to blame Bishop for the shooting, sent him hard looks where he stood apart by his horse.

Don Ricardo strolled from the chapel, inquiring whether Kerry Dyal had been given notice to dress and prepare for travel.

The men glanced at one another. No one had thought of it in the process of making up what amounted to a baggage train. He frowned, mounting the horse that was saddled for him, a silvery palomino.

"I'll attend to it." His frown was for Bishop. He said to him crisply across the yard, "Stay here, or ride off, as you wish. Don't follow us! We'll drop you on sight! You don't have a rifle. I have"—he slapped the polished stock protruding from its scabbard—"and my men have their carbines! Fair warning?"

49

Bishop nodded, and watched him start down to the village. A fairer warning than he might have expected from Rico in his present brittle mood. He switched his regard to the eight waiting men. No warning from them, if and when they decided to try conclusions.

The jogging beat of the palomino broke into a fast stamping. Don Ricardo had suddenly wheeled the horse and was racing back up the hill. Shots hammered out before he reached the gap in the mission wall, lifting the palomino in a tremendous leap that brought it crashing into the gap in an end-over-end tangle.

The Don sailed outspread, but hunched himself in time to take a rolling fall. He sprang up spitting dirt, found his guns and hat, and yelled something that was lost in the uproar, his men by then firing over the wall.

Bishop shouted to him, "How many, Rico?"

"God knows!" he shouted back. "I only got a glimpse."

"Told you that joker would soon be back with friends!"

"Damn you, Rogue! I had a good thing here until you turned up!"

The shooting slackened and one of the men called out, "They're falling back!"

Bishop peered over the wall. The attackers were huddled shadows crawling in retreat down the long slope. As they reached the foot of it, one by one they rose and went flitting around the hill. "They're making for the village!" he rasped, and jumped to his horse.

Riding through the gap, he spied the foremost of them, two figures sprinting, then others trailing hard behind. Having parted with their horses, they were clearly out to take the village and fort up in it. Their creeping attack on the mission had failed, launched too soon because Don Ricardo spotted them. Or it could have been a feint, Bishop thought. They hadn't pressed it very strenuously.

He threw two shots at the two leading figures. They dived to earth, but he doubted that he had hit them. Darkness and distance and the jolting saddle combined to make shooting chancy. A rifle lashed at him. Others joined in, lancing the night with flashes and the rattling whines of bullets, and he veered off. He had brought the running men to halt for the moment, and that was so much to the good.

He stretched the dun out, clattered into the village, and hauled in before the adobe house occupied by Kerry Dyal and her chaperone. No lights showed and only a few muffled sounds

50

told that the shooting had awakened the village. The door of the house was fastened, and figuring it wouldn't be opened willingly to him, he crashed it in with his shoulder.

Horses came sweeping down the hill from the mission and gunfire rose again, rifles in the majority. The men on foot hadn't put up much of a fight before, but they were hard at it now, shooting it out with the Don and his men. A horse screamed, and leathers popped in the crunch of a collision. Bishop ducked into the house, calling, "Kerry Dyal! Come on—got to get out of here!"

"Quién va?"

He blundered into the woman in the dark, and reaching to save her from a fall, his hand batted her and completed her tumble. She screeched, floundering among the furniture. A white-clad figure darted across the room like a ghost, crying, "Brigida, Brigida! Where's your gun?"

He was all against letting Kerry Dyal get her hands on a gun, so he promptly swooped at her, picked her up bodily, and headed at once for the door. She screamed, fighting him with surprising strength. The woman hollered, calling on all the saints and Don Ricardo to save her young mistress from the brutal villain who bashed into homes and knocked down women.

Outside, he swore at the dun for shying away from him and his struggling bundle. At the edge of the village the fight raged on, moving closer. The Don and his men seemed now to be on the defensive. A man on foot burst out from a yard, raising his rifle and staring about him. Bishop had his hands full of Kerry Dyal. He freed his right hand by tucking her under his left arm, and fired a shot that sent the rifleman stumbling back into the yard. The dun shied again.

Hanging onto Kerry Dyal, he caught up the reins and managed to climb into the saddle and straighten the horse out. The route north out of the village was barred by the shooters, and he set off southward, figuring to circle around the hill and backtrack north while Rico and his men were kept busy, but as he quit the village he heard them pounding after him. His hope that they would delay themselves at the house went flittering too, for the woman there rattled off a stream of words at them and they came on without halting.

Kerry Dyal kept flailing with her arms and legs, doing him no particular hurt but unsettling the dun's temper. "If I drop you now," he told her, "you'll feel it! Behave yourself and I'll let you sit up like a lady." He swung her up before him, his left arm clamped around her. It wasn't the easiest seat for her, no padding, but better than dangling. "You're safe, don't worry!"

"I was safe with Mr. de Risa!"

"Matter of opinion!"

His horse broke its gait and lost headway during the transfer, and behind him Don Ricardo rapped out, "Pull up, Rogue, we have a horse for her!" Bitterly he added, "More horses than men!" He raced up alongside, riding a black-and-white paint.

"Wait till we get round the hill," Bishop countered, edging off. The next instant he hauled the dun up rearing. "Look out!"

Dead ahead riders bore down on them. Don Ricardo slung his horse around and a gun roared in his hand. His men in the rear stamped to a jumbled halt, uncertain of what course to take. He called, "Get her away, Rogue—we'll cover!"

With the advancing riders spreading out in front and the riflemen coming from the village behind, and the hill on the left, there was only one way open. Bishop lined the dun westward, heeling it hard, leaving the shooting to freer hands than his own. In a tight scrape he couldn't wish for a more free-handed scrapper at his back than Rico.

The line of riders opened up like an efficient cavalry squad, firing to drive the outnumbered enemy back toward the village and the riflemen. It was plain that the two parties were working as one, following a maneuver that had been designed to draw Don Ricardo and his men out into the open and annihilate them. Their timing had gone askew only by minutes and they were out to repair that mischance.

Two end-riders swung over to head Bishop off. He gave ground rather than juggle a gun, and lifting his horse to an extra burst of speed he skinned by. They fired after he passed. Their shots hit the ground and bounced off droning. They had sighted Kerry Dyal's white dress and were aiming low at the dun to bring it down. At their urgent hail the riders all wheeled in pursuit. He hoped Rico could do something about that.

They rested their horses in a chaparral crotch between open ridges. A breeze sprang up and died, coyotes howled their dawn chorus, then the sun rose and all was quiet and still.

One of Don Ricardo's three remaining men climbed down

from a ridge to report a plume of dust toward the south, evidently moving along their tracks. He added that the Rio Grande was in sight, empty of life.

Bishop said, "We won't shake them off this side of the river. They've got us backed up. These horses don't have a good run left in them, and we're low on shells. And Kerry needs clothes."

"A pity you didn't see to that before you carried her out of the house!" Don Ricardo observed.

"It was dark and I didn't think of it."

They gazed at her thoughtfully. She wore a white night-gown over which was draped a Mexican saddle-blanket striped blood-red and bile-green, robbed off a spare horse. Her feet were bare and her hair hung free as a mane. The effect was more exotic than practical.

"I'm no more attracted back to Texas than you are, Rico," Bishop admitted. "We're both posted there. But here we're dead ducks! Must have been fifteen or twenty of those jokers last night. They can get more!"

"Hired with Hatchet money, you think?"

"Pretty sure of it. I say we mosey up to the Hill Country, get the county sheriff—"

"No sheriff!"

"She'll need him for protection on Hatchet."

Don Ricardo walked off a few paces, motioning for Bishop to follow. Out of Kerry Dyal's hearing, he said, "You are interested in protecting her. So am I. We are interested in money, too, but would Dyal pay us for delivering her alive?" He shook his head. "No, I have a better idea. Kill Dyal, and Kerry inherits Hatchet as his next of kin!"

"Not if there's a half-brother living. Dyal's first-born."

"We'll attend to him, too, if he shows up!"

As usual, the Don had hit upon a logically sound solution, disregarding the morals of murder. "If she owned Hatchet she'd be safe, all right," Bishop conceded.

"Safe as a queen!" Don Ricardo said brightly. "We can do it, Rogue! And with me there as her business manager, adviser, friend, and protector—"

"You?" Bishop eyed him bleakly. "You'd strip Hatchet to the grassroots! No, Rico, we'll scout a bit and size things up when we get there. I'm not sure about old man Dyal. You never met him. Tough old rawhide. Didn't strike me he'd fool about hiring any stranger to kill his daughter for him. Kill her himself if he had to!"

"So?"

"So if it works out straight we collect five thousand, split it even, and vamoose."

The cynical glint in Don Ricardo's eyes said that splitting the loot was difficult for him to imagine. But he nodded, his face innocent. "We go by way of Carrizo Springs and Bandera, staying off the main roads, eh?"

"Yeah, and let your hombres trail way behind us. "They're good hombres, but bad company. Any Texas lawman'd spot 'em for border jumpers and think we're the same."

"Lord forbid!"

"It's going to be damned awkward as it is, three hundred miles dodging Rangers and such. Let's get going. You break the news to Kerry we're heading for Hatchet just for her sake. She trusts you, Lord help her!"

SEVEN

The McLaughlin Emporium in Carrizo Springs stocked a vast assortment of goods. Carrizo Springs lay well off the traveled stageroads, but it catered to ranchmen for thirty miles around and was a supply point for trail outfits starting north up the Nueces. It had three saloons, one of them—the Palm House—fully equipped with the conveniences of gambling tables and painted Lulus.

The emporium was long and narrow. An aisle ran through it, on both sides of which were piled loads of ham, bacon, salt pork, sacks of flour, corn, sugar, coffee in hundred-pound boxes, molasses, baking powder, soda, knocked-down Bain and Shuttler wagons, harness, horseshoes, Dutch ovens, and a thousand other necessities. In all the welter of goods, though, female apparel was in short supply.

The storekeeper, keeping his eyes carefully averted from Kerry Dyal after his first startled look at her nightgown, explained primly to Bishop and Don Ricardo that women bought dress goods and made up their own.

"They sew in the saddle?" Don Ricardo asked. "Clever!"

The storekeeper sniffed. He left unspoken his opinion of a pair of pistoleros riding up from the border with a girl who had left her clothes behind. They were cash customers, buying shells and a stock of grub for the road. "Some women call in a dressmaker to help. There's a little woman, Miz Pemberthy, who—"

"Take too long," Bishop said.

"I got some calico gowns Miz Pemberthy made up, only they're all the same size, about, an'—"

"Why'n't you say so? Look 'em over, Kerry."

They paid their bills while Kerry made her selection and tried it on somewhere in the rear. The storekeeper's stiff manner indicated it was the first time the emporium had ever been used as a lady's dressing room and he didn't approve of it. He counted their money twice, inspecting it with a suspicion that hinted he thought it might be counterfeit. Stolen, at any rate.

"Have no doubts of our honesty," Don Ricardo assured him loftily. "My friend is a Bishop."

"I bet!"

"You are a betting man? Ah! Then—"

"Lay off, Rico!" Bishop growled. The Don was regaining his old sense of humor. All very well, but too often it became a twisted sense of humor that carried him into a spirit of mischief. Especially in Texas where people were apt to eye intolerantly his charro garb and take as an affront his jaunty manner. Texans still remembered the Alamo. He brought out the prejudice in them, and they brought out the devil in him.

"Then," Don Ricardo continued imperturbably, "I will bet you—" He broke off as Kerry Dyal came forth from the rear of the emporium. His face underwent changing expressions from astonishment to hilarity. Bishop couldn't restrain a grin.

The calico gown was a shapeless affair of unfortunate brown, verging on stale mustard, fashioned to the proportions of a six-foot being of phenomenal girth. Obviously it was unfinished, intended to be taken in, taken up, refitted to the wearer. To fit Kerry, more than half of it needed whacking off. It hung on her in folds and trailed behind her. She dimly resembled an infant in swaddling clothes of poor quality, taking a precocious amble.

She flushed painfully at Don Ricardo's laughter and Bishop's grin. It was the first reaction Bishop had seen in her of truly feminine self-consciousness, outside of her embarrassment about the nightgown. He wiped off his grin and scowled at Don Ricardo.

"Maybe some fixing here and there—"

"No, no!" the Don choked. "Take it off, *querida*—take it off!" He reached to a fold of it. She jumped back, and he withdrew his hand. *"Mil perdones!"*

"Keep it on till we work something out," Bishop told her, some of his usual harshness absent from his voice. She looked to be on the edge of tears. "It covers you, anyhow."

"You won't find nothing better'n that in Carrizo Springs!" declared the storekeeper resentfully. "It's good-wearin' calico!"

"I bet I can!" said the Don, starting out.

"Step light, Rico!" Bishop called after him. "Don't stir up anything!" They had eased quietly into the town and left their horses alongside the emporium, unobtrusively off the

56

street. To the storekeeper he said, "Open a can of peaches for the lady. Got any whiskey?"

"Barrel, jug, or bottle?"

"Gallon jug." No telling when they'd enter another town, and it was rattlesnake country. He watched the storekeeper fill the jug from a barrel and drive the cork in with a thump that meant no drinking on these premises. A dry Baptist, likely. Kerry ate the canned peaches. He caught her glancing seriously at him, and he turned a smile for her. She dropped her eyes, but the second time she smiled back, uncertainly. Like Rico, he wondered what her laughter sounded like. If she ever laughed.

Don Ricardo returned bearing a colorful bundle. He handed it to Kerry with a swaggering bow. "A new dress and, er, all the necessary accoutrements! Never been worn. The Palm House lady was saving it for a special event. Her trousseau, I think."

"You steal it?" Bishop asked him.

He drew himself up. "I paid a fortune for it, almost a queen's ransom! Let beauty be suitably adorned at all costs!"

Kerry, inspecting the adornment, fingered a velvet bodice or emerald green, studded all over with some kind of sparklers. There seemed to be a flame-red skirt to go with it, and a considerable amount of lace. She gazed speechlessly from Don Ricardo to Bishop.

"Might's well try it on," Bishop said. Just like Rico to buy a Lulu's outfit for her. His taste for extravagant raiment. Nothing cheap about him, nor conservative. At that, the outfit might serve as a disguise. Particularly if she painted her face to match. A Lulu riding with a pair of . . .

It occurred to Bishop that Rico, smart as he was, couldn't have done his buying without news of the unusual transaction spreading all over town, drawing notice to them. "Hurry!" he urged Kerry, and she retreated to the rear, an odd little figure in the oversize calico wrapper and her arms full of finery.

He chose a couple of wool blankets from a stack and added them to his purchases. "Gets cool at night up in the Hill Country," he mentioned, "and that get-up you bought her doesn't look warm."

Don Ricardo smiled. "It may not feel warm," he corrected, "but it will *look* warm!"

"How many know you bought it?"

"There were a few in the barroom, staring and listening.

57

These people lead such humdrum lives, they're inquisitive about anything uncommon. Here comes the first one." Don Ricardo nodded contemptuously toward the front window. "Hungry with idle curiosity!"

The man passing the window slowed down, looking in. His look was sharp. He passed the open doorway. His boots and clothes were dusty. He wore a gun. Two more men sauntered angling across the street, seemingly uninterested in everything but their saloon cigars. They too bore the dust of very recent travel, as if just in off the trail. Hard travel, that had sweat-soaked their shirts around the beltline and beneath the armpits.

"Idle curiosity?" Bishop muttered. "Idle, Rico? Look again!"

"Those weren't in the Palm House, Rogue! Damn! Do you—"

"There's another! I know that one. He was with the five that picked up my horse way south of San Antonio."

They watched, counting the men emerging onto the street, trying to figure which were there out of curiosity, which were not.

"News spreads fast here!"

The storekeeper made a gulping sound, and they turned their heads. Kerry was coming down the aisle to the front. The velvet bodice fitted her pretty well. A bit loose at the waist, but filled out above. The flame-red skirt flared out, lace petticoats beneath, to display her ankles. Her shoes were of the same emerald-green velvet as the bodice, and also sparkler-trimmed.

"Well!" Don Ricardo breathed. "She—she's—did you ever see such—"

"Not often," said Bishop. "You forgot her hat." She had tied back her hair with a red ribbon, a touch of simplicity which was all that disqualified her as a ripe young dance-hall queen.

The Don snapped his fingers. "So I did!"

"Some other time, amigo." Bishop returned his regard to the street. "How about you go take the horses round to the back? Act like you don't know the score. I'll head 'em off if they start after you."

"Bien!"

Seeing him start for the rear, the thought entered Bishop's head that he and Rico were in some ways much alike. In Mexico he tended to give Rico first voice, and north of the

58

border Rico inclined to defer to him, although they both knew their way about in both lands.

"Kerry," he said, "bundle our stuff up in the blankets and carry it to the back door. Wait there inside till Rico comes round with the horses. When it's time to go, move fast!"

She looked up into his face, studying his eyes as she had done before. The sense of emergency drove out the self-consciousness that she obviously felt about her apparel. "What's the matter?"

"Some of the men we got away from are out there." He jerked his chin toward the sun-glared street. "Tracked us here, or guessed our route. Not sure how many."

"Men my father hired?"

"Not sure of that either. I do know they're out to get us, and that's enough for now. Just do like I say, eh?"

She hesitated before slowly backing away, still gazing at him. The storekeeper came forward, flapping both his hands.

"Say, there! You get outside if there's going to be any fighting! I got breakable goods in here!"

"You got a breakable head, too!" Bishop growled. "Stand out of her way!"

He turned to the street. Across a patch of it that he could see through the open door two men moved in response to a whistle, making to cut around the emporium. Somebody must have spotted Rico easing out to the horses. Another man lounged after them, paused as if lazily changing his mind, and came on over to the emporium boardwalk. His figure loomed up against the front window and sank out of sight as he seated himself under it in the shade.

Of the men now visible in the street, Bishop judged that none was there out of idle curiosity. The curious ones had taken in the signs of preparation, and bowed to prudence. He stepped forward to the doorway. The two hurrying men sent sidelong looks at him, but they kept on toward the horses, leaving him to be attended to by others. The man sitting beneath the window jerked up his head. Two more men, standing by the hitching rack in front of the Palm House farther down the street, shifted indolently forward at sight of him.

He waited, eyes swinging left to right and back, until the two hurrying men, showing definitely their purpose, almost reached the mouth of the alley alongside the emporium. He sent a quiet demand at them.

"Where you going?"

They stopped short. Both made the half-turn slowly and

59

laid deliberating stares on him. One, a gaunt man with lines of fatigue etching his face, lowered tired eyes to Bishop's hands.

The other, younger, square-faced and bold-eyed, took his cigar from his mouth and sent twin spears of blue smoke through his nostrils. The act of a grandstander. "Any business of yours?"

"It is," Bishop murmured. "You know it is!" He shifted slightly to keep the squatting man partly in his view. The man was close to him, barely five feet on his right.

"Well, now!" The young man took another puff on his cigar. He put on an exaggerated look of pondering. "Don't see how it could be. No sir. Don't see how. We're—"

The whistle cut shrilly through the quietness. It shattered the sluggish pattern of the street. In a split second the younger man exchanged his cigar for a gun. The gaunt man was only a shade behind.

Bishop made his cross-draw while dropping to one knee, and fired. His bullet took the younger man in his shooting arm and slung him across the trunk of his partner, who promptly used him for cover. Bishop slapped out his second gun and fired again. The gaunt man, weaving his thin body like a snake standing on its tail, trying for a safe shot behind his swaying cover, lurched out broken-legged and threw down his gun.

Bishop slid around on his knee. The two men from the Palm House hitching rack were coming at a sprint, guns up. Under the lower edge of the saloon's batwing doors, a man lay hastily lining up a rifle.

But it was the man squatting beneath the emporium window, five feet away, who had the drop. The blue glint of his gun barrel shrank to the muzzle, aimed point-blank. Bishop slashed around with his right-hand gun, knowing he had neglected that fellow too long.

The emporium window burst outward. The sudden crash of it startled the two sprinting men into dodging aside as if a bomb had exploded, and shook a premature shot from the rifle under the batwing doors.

Broken glass showered down on the squatting man. Something bounced off his head and smashed in the street. He rocked forward and his shot snarled by Bishop's face.

Don Ricardo's voice, loud and cool, rang out from the back. "Come on, Rogue! Stop your fooling and let's ride!"

Bishop threw one more shot and rolled back into the doorway. He bounded up and found Kerry Dyal only a few steps ahead of him down the aisle, their bundle of purchases a bulky burden under her arm.

"Damn it, I told you to go to the back door and wait there!" he snapped at her, and hurried her along.

They raced through the emporium. The back door, open, gave a glimpse of Don Ricardo holding the reins of their three saddled horses, laughing as he peered in.

"Hey, you!" The storekeeper bobbed his head up from behind a pile of merchandise. "Come back here! You got to pay me for that window! And you didn't pay me for the whiskey! You can't—"

"See you next trip," Bishop said, and loped on, pushing Kerry ahead of him. They bolted out back and he lifted her onto her horse. Somebody, somewhere, was firing wild. Probably the man with the rifle.

"Window and the whiskey!" the storekeeper howled, "Gotta pay me! I'll have the law—!"

"What the hell's he talking about?" Bishop growled, grabbing up his reins and taking a hasty glance at Kerry's bundle. "We left the whiskey behind."

"I'll swear to that!" Don Ricardo chuckled. He nodded his head at Kerry. "She owes for it, though. She used it all. I saw her swing that jug and heave it through the window at a hand that had a gun in it aimed at you. Wish I could have seen what it did to that hombre—must have been funny!"

"So that was it!" Bishop caught up Kerry's reins. She was holding onto the bundle. "I wondered. You saw it, eh, Rico? You just stood and looked on. Couldn't pick a shot at that hand, I suppose. Or could you?"

"Oh, yes," Don Ricardo replied blandly. "But you were doing all right, amigo. And you had her to help you. She learns fast! Is that blood on your neck?"

Bishop touched it. "It's not whiskey. Bullet skinned me."

They raced by the rear ends of the buildings along the main street. A rifle cracked as they passed an empty gap. Don Ricardo's sombrero tipped over on his nose. He swore, righted it, and looked back. "Up on a roof, that one! They didn't intend us to get out of this town! And we haven't come a quarter of the way yet. Let's hope their horses are no fresher than ours."

They put Carrizo Springs behind them and turned off to the Nueces. Observing no pursuers, they slowed gait to save their horses. The one advantage they possessed was that they could dodge and cover their tracks, hiding out when weariness demanded, while the hunters had to use up their horses cutting for sign. The advantage was weakened by the fact that their destination was known to the hunters, who clearly didn't intend them to reach it.

Don Ricardo lit a cigarette and inhaled deeply. "I hope my three hombres avoid that town! Sad, if they rode in trustingly and were blasted out of their saddles!"

"They won't. You've got 'em trailing that close behind us they couldn't help hear the shooting. They might come in handy at Bandera. We've got enough grub to last us there. By then we'll be out of grain for the horses. That Bandera's a tougher town than Carrizo Springs. From there it's a long day's ride to Hatchet, rough country all the way."

Kerry cried suddenly. "Let's give it up!"

She was riding between them and they both looked at her and met each other's eyes. "Can't turn back now," Bishop said shortly.

"Don't take me back to Hatchet!"

He sighed. Her fear was so real. And he couldn't say it wasn't well founded. For all he knew, Simon Dyal had murdered her mother, planned to murder her, and hired an unknown number of gunmen to track down and kill her present guardians. "We'll look over the setup first," he told her. "If it's not right, we'll not leave you there. That's a promise."

"On your oath?"

He nodded. "You've got to trust us." Saying that made him feel as false as Rico, and he sent him a baleful stare. But Rico's eyes were solemn, not mocking nor cynical.

"Yes, try to trust us. We'll not sell you out." Don Ricardo flipped away the stub of his cigarette. "We're good men, aren't we, Rogue?"

"Good in some ways."

"But I'm the better man!"

"The hell you say!" Bishop said it casually. Then the quiet ring in Rico's voice caught in his ear, and he looked swiftly at him and saw cold earnestness. He thought of Rico standing back in the emporium while he himself made a kneeling target for a leveled gun at point-blank range. Kerry, heaving the whiskey jug through the window, had proved herself ready to stick by him. He guessed that hadn't pleased Rico too much.

Jealousy. She wasn't much more than a child, though

62

that was hard to remember, seeing her now in those clothes. Rico was twice her age in years, a hundred times in experience. A thousand times.

The thought came unbidden: *So am I.*

EIGHT

They stayed out of Bandera; were able to because Don Ricardo's three men caught up with them and the Don sent them in for the necessary grain and grub. He warned them to ride in singly, on the *cuidado,* and slip out again. They swore to be discreet, circumspect, making no more ripple than three mice.

They returned riding like the furies, driving a bunch of saddled horses before them. Their hasty excuse was that certain men had approached them with evil intent, demanding to know where they came from and where they were going—impertinently personal questions which no self-respecting *hombre del campo* could fail to resent.

It happened in a saloon which they entered by mistake, they said, and after laying about with their carbines they ran into a man wearing a badge who wanted to arrest them. That would have caused Don Ricardo much inconvenience on account of the grain and grub, so they clouted the man down. The town then turned against them. To delay pursuit they spooked all the horses in the street and brought them along. Indeed, Bandera was not a friendly town.

"Not now anyhow," Bishop said. "We might as well change to fresh horses while we can." He was piling up a considerable score of wrongdoings in Texas and a stolen horse more or less didn't make any difference.

They changed horses, scattered the rest, and rode on, the Don rebuking his men and they protesting their blamelessness.

Kerry was getting a drawn look, Bishop noted. She wasn't made for this kind of life. The nearer they got to Hatchet the more solemn she became. She trusted him and Rico, but they and Rico's men made only five against Hatchet and against the pursuing gunmen hired by Hatchet money. Rico's men, for all their dependable combativeness, weren't too reliable when it came to carrying out patient hide-and-seek tactics. Too apt to blow the cork, as in Bandera. Innocent and gullible as Kerry might be, Bishop gave her credit for having the clear sense to see that the prospect was worse than desperate.

"Our one chance," he said aloud, "is to look up the county sheriff. She'll be safe with him."

"By this time the county sheriff is most likely out looking for us!" Don Ricardo responded icily. "She is safe with us as long as we're safe."

"That may not be long!"

Don Ricardo twisted his lips. "Nerves, Rogue?"

Bishop ignored the gibe. "We'll reach Hatchet sometime tonight at this rate," he said. "These horses will be spent. In the morning guns will be sprouting all over Hatchet! They'll know we got there."

"They'll know," Don Ricardo assented, "because we'll strike tonight!"

Silent for a while, Bishop said finally, "The summer work's on. What hands Hatchet can spare won't be many. I'm not counting the guns behind us. They won't be far behind."

"That's why we must strike tonight," Don Ricardo pointed out. "After tonight will be too late."

"All right, we can figure it's known at Hatchet that we're on our way. They could even have an idea of when we'll get there. Messengers from those jokers behind us can ride straight there in a hurry, picking up fresh horses on the way, while we've had to lose time antigodlin around the brush and holeing up at night. Hatchet will be ready for us!"

"You make it sound impossible," Don Ricardo said.

Bishop shook his head. "No, I'm looking past my nose. Try it sometime. Hatchet hands—meaning Osterberg and some others—will be on the watch for us. My guess is they'll have orders to stop us from getting to the home ranch. It's what the guns behind us have been trying to do."

"Perhaps we can find out," Don Ricardo suggested. "On the road to Hatchet there's a little place called Forks—"

"I've been there. Sorta Hatchet's town."

"If you're right, they'd be sure to have a man or two posted there. *If* you're right. We'll take a look."

"That could just be what they figure we'll do," Bishop said. "They know we won't ride up neighborly on the home ranch and hail the house!"

Don Ricardo made an explosive sound. "You object to everything! What do you propose?"

"Look up the county sheriff and—"

"No! You look him up if you wish. Give yourself up and be

65

damned to you! As for me, I go to Forks, to Hatchet, and do what I set out to do!" His irritable vehemence hinted at an underlying doubt, an unsureness that was rare in him. Something was gnawing at his daredevil tenacity. Not Bishop's words. Something else.

By night, Forks was no town at all, only a clapboard saloon at a crossroads, a few vague outbuildings in the background. Stars and a yellow crescent of moon low in a blue-black sky let it conceal its drabness. The saloon's lighted windows, lifeless of any moving shadows, shone on an empty hitching rack.

Don Ricardo said, using a word he seldom employed, "Gringo cowtowns! The smaller they are the more ugly!" He moved restlessly in his saddle. "Why does that *cantinero* keep his lights on so late?" It was long past midnight. "He has no customers."

"Maybe he's expecting some," Bishop said.

They sat their mounts on a rise overlooking the Hatchet road and gazed down at Forks. Don Ricardo's three men huddled in their serapes, finding the night air of the Hill Country too cool for comfort.

"It's too dead," Bishop said. He wondered if his nose for trouble was side-tracking him, bending him toward overcaution. Then noticing the Don's restlessness, he knew what it was. They both were uneasy for the same reason, and the reason was Kerry Dyal.

The Don sent him a look, mockery glimmering in his dark eyes. "Nerves!" He threw back his shoulders, tipped his head arrogantly. "Nerves, Rogue! You need a drink. Why don't you drop down and stir up the *cantinero?* He must be lonely for company."

Bishop shook his head thoughtfully. "I don't need a drink that much. If the place is as dead as it looks, we might push on and scout Hatchet. I could be wrong about them waiting for us."

"You could," Don Ricardo said. "But a feeling grows in me that you're right. As you say, they must know we got clear of their pistoleros. They must be expecting us."

"And so—?" Bishop let the rest of the question hang.

"I'm changing my mind about this thing." Don Ricardo turned his head and looked directly at Kerry. "About going on to Hatchet."

"Now we're so close to it? You're a bit late!"

"Not too late!"

"Nerves, Rico?" Bishop murmured.

"Logic!" retorted Don Ricardo. "This idea of yours was wrong from the start! We should never have brought Kerry back here. Simon Dyal wants her dead. Knowing we're in the country, he'll keep himself too heavily guarded for us to get at. Kerry must be protected from him, not taken into a Hatchet death trap!"

"Are you sure your interest in her is only protective?" Bishop queried.

The Don ignored the question. He said, "Even if we did get Dyal, then what? We'd still have the law on our necks! It's going to be hard getting out of Texas as it is!"

"I thought Kerry was your main concern. She'd be safe."

"Would she? The damn law would probably charge her with complicity in the murder of her own father! I wouldn't leave her to face that." What he meant was, Bishop knew, he would not part with Kerry. That was what accounted for his growing restlessness and proddy temper.

Kerry shivered. "Let's give it up!" she said once more, and again they both looked at her. She was white-faced in the darkness.

"Rico," Bishop said, "there are some things you don't know about this caper. And some things I don't know. Before I throw it in, I want a word with Dyal."

"About Kerry?"

"About her, and about her half-brother. And Frank Wittrock. And Owl Osterberg. And two or three other matters. Let's go!"

Don Ricardo shook his head. "You go! Not Kerry!" He leaned toward her. "I'll take you back to Mexico. You would prefer that to Hatchet, wouldn't you?"

She hesitated, turning her face again to Bishop, then back again. "Yes, but—"

"Of course you would!" Don Ricardo stroked her shoulder. "You see, Rogue? The choice is hers, not yours! What can you do? Not a damn—" His teeth clicked shut. His right hand stopped its quick downward stroke.

Bishop had his right arm laid across his waist. He whipped a rapid glance at the Don's three men, shrunk morosely under their serapes. "Do?" he whispered savagely. His deep-set eyes stabbed naked menace. "I can blow a hole through you!"

They glared into each other's eys. The Don dipped another swift look at the bulge in Bishop's coat poking at him.

"I've always known you had a mad streak! It comes out at the strangest times."

"And your woman itch comes out any time! A red skirt and a pair of ankles and you're a prancing Lothario!" Bishop said it for Kerry to hear. "How long would she last? How many like her have you got tired of?"

"None like her." Perhaps at the moment Don Ricardo believed it himself. A new woman was always the only one for him—until the next.

"You're a liar!"

"Careful! Don't—"

"What's it to be?" Bishop cut in.

"If you shoot me, you'll have to take on my men. End of the game!"

"It's up to you!"

Don Ricardo took out a flat silver case, extracted a black cigarette, and returned the case to his jacket pocket. His hands were steady, unhurried. With the cigarette between his lips, and a match poised, he looked down meditatively at the lighted windows.

"You're dealing, Rogue." He nodded sideways at the bulge. "But I'm calling the play. I propose we buy a drink down there and see if we can find out what Hatchet is doing. Hombres!"

The three came alive, quickly alert, as if the ring to his voice conveyed more to them than the single word, much more. He slapped Kerry's horse lightly on the flank and nudged forward his own.

"You're dealing, Rogue!" he repeated over his shoulder as they dropped down the slope toward Forks. "It would be useless to advise you to drop out. Advice is wasted on you."

"From you, every bit!"

"Too bad! I don't see how we'll get along, do you?"

Bishop didn't. He slid his gun back in its holster. He couldn't hold Rico at gunpoint every instant. Rico's men were aware of the drastic break between them; they rode well apart, holding him under somber regard and maneuvering to fall behind him. To circumvent them he had to keep checking his horse. So it was that Don Ricardo and Kerry reached the crossroads ahead of him.

Don Ricardo had helped Kerry dismount with a gallant

68

flourish and was walking her to the saloon doors when Bishop drew up.

"Are you taking her in there, Rico?"

At Bishop's question, he turned, eyebrows raised. "Would you have me leave her outside?" He motioned to his men to stay back.

Bishop swept a look over the three. Whatever signal had passed between them and Rico, it had brought them up out of their lethargy. He didn't care to let Rico out of his sight, and at the same time he wasn't going to have Kerry wait outside with them, or they'd probably be off with her by Rico's unspoken command.

Stumped, he said, "I reckon not."

"She is dressed suitably!" The Don paid her a bow. She had worn a blanket over her finery, and he had removed it as if it were a precious cloak. "She will bring cheer to this dreary dive! But if you object, Rogue—"

"Go on in, you dirty twister!"

"Rogue"—Don Ricardo paused at the saloon doors— "I usually play for all the stakes, as you do! That was between us when this was a matter of money. But there is no more Hatchet money forthcoming. There is only Kerry. I'll not let you take her, and we certainly won't share her!"

He shoved open the saloon doors.

"So we will have a drink," he said, smiling. "But I think it will be our last drink together!"

They stepped into the barroom, a silent barn of a place with an unswept floor and a bar built of plain boards. Behind the bar, under hanging oil lamps, a bartender leaned in an attitude of endless patience. Bald and fat and sleepy, he raised slow-moving eyes to the incoming three, and yawned. The sight of Kerry drew from him no more evidence of surprise than if girls in flamboyant dresses daily paraded through Forks.

Rico glanced at the bottles on the backbar shelves. "Whiskey for me, seeing you have nothing else. Do you drink, Kerry?"

She shook her head.

"Whiskey," Bishop said. He scanned the empty barroom. A curl of smoke caught his eye. The stub of a cigarette burned on the edge of a table. On the same table stood a few partly finished drinks. *"Cuidado!"* he murmured.

"H'm?" Rico was examining distastefully the cloudy glass set before him. He polished it fastidiously with his handkerchief before filling it from the bottle.

Bishop scanned farther afield. There was a door off to the left, open, darkness beyond. Cardroom, he guessed, or a room for storage. The bar lamps sent a long yellow triangle through the open door and across the floor of the unlighted room.

"A slow night, eh?" Rico remarked to the bartender. He turned and glanced at the front window. Its lower half was protected by nailed planks.

"Slow," the bartender grunted, and withdrew unsociably along the bar.

"I shouldn't think it would be worth the lamp oil to stay open," Don Ricardo pursued. "Are you expecting some trade?"

He got no answer.

Bishop poured his whiskey, his eyes on the triangle of light. He, too, turned so that he had a view of the front window. He shot a swift look at it, wondering if Rico's men were behind the nailed planks, peering through the crevices. When he looked again at the triangle of light, its outline was broken.

He finished filling his glass, put the bottle behind him on the bar, and eyed the man who stepped slowly out from the darkened room. Owl Osterberg. Bishop sent him a nod. The Hatchet range boss returned the nod, his staring round eyes expressionless. He moved to the table and sat down facing the bar, keeping his chair pushed back, hands in his lap.

Don Ricardo shifted to place Kerry on his left, and this brought him next to Bishop. "Good evening, Osterberg!" he said lightly, entirely untroubled on the surface, unabashed at facing the man who, as go-between, had engaged him to abduct Kerry and whose orders he had blatantly double-crossed.

Owl Osterberg shifted his eyes to him and on to Kerry. He gave her no sign of recognition.

Other men came drifting out of the darkened room. Jay Nunn. Eben Dekker. Colorado George. They, too, feigned not to know Kerry. Two more followed, then another pair. Bishop knew them only as the riders who trailed him out of San Antonio down to Laredo. They didn't come up to the bar. They ranged themselves quietly along the walls of the barroom like men come to meeting. Had they removed their hats they might have been in court.

Bishop sipped his drink, wondering what the move was to be, and whether the presence of Kerry was delaying it. They knew her as well as they knew old man Dyal, but were following Osterberg's lead in pretending blank ignorance of her identity.

He waited for some reaction from Don Ricardo and when none came he murmured, "Is this your doing, Rico? Did you know what we were getting into here?"

"Lord, no!" Don Ricardo whispered. "I had something else planned." His eyes skimmed over the front window.

"Your hombres can't do much out there! If they start anything we'll have one hell of a bust-up in here! Damn you, I had a feeling Forks might be loaded! I hope you get blasted to hell!"

"I'll have company!"

Bishop took a deep breath. "Kerry," he muttered, "walk to the door. Don't run till you get outside, then jump on your horse and scoot! Find the county sheriff. Go ahead! Ready, Rico?"

"Ready!"

The girl hesitated, looking at both of them with her grave eyes. Slowly, she moved away from them and started across the floor. Bishop found time to admire her self-control. She walked easily, unhurriedly.

Osterberg spoke for the first time. "Girl, come here!"

The rough force that weighted his voice stopped her for an instant. She froze, then started forward again.

"Girl!"

That time she ignored his command and walked on steadily. Colorado George and two others nearest the doors stepped swiftly to bar her way and round her in.

"Now, Lulu, you heard the man!" Colorado George drawled.

She had to halt then or walk into them. Bishop took a short step forward from the bar, aware that Don Ricardo was pacing away from his side, letting him take up the play.

"Let her pass," he snapped at Colorado George.

Osterberg rose from the table. "Wait a minute. That girl—" Like a stage magician distracting attention from a deft bit of palming, he raised his right hand to point to her, and stroked fast with his left to the holster on his hip. That was the signal for other hands to slap down on gun butts. The men stilled, their eyes mocking Bishop for losing the edge.

Don Ricardo had circled to come up behind Kerry, and Osterberg side-stepped from the table, his left arm rigid, fingers closed on his half-drawn gun. "De Risa, stop right there!" he commanded. His staring eyes never left Bishop. "You got something to say?"

Bishop nodded. "You've got a tight setup here, Owl, but it won't fall your way. Let the girl go. We'll—"

"Rogue Bishop—asking for terms!" Osterberg broke in and almost smiled. "De Risa—trying to run out! Boys, these are the ring-tailed scorchers who gave you all the trouble! A broken-down pair of gun pilgrims—"

Don Ricardo let out an ear-splitting yell and his shoulder hit Kerry from behind, hurling her past Colorado George and on out through the swing doors. It was a rough exit for Kerry, but effectively fast. The doors stayed open after she plunged through, caught and held by Don Ricardo's three men outside. For a moment the three stood there in line, firing their carbines at waist level.

Bishop snatched out his guns, dodging low as the carbines roared high into the barroom. Above and behind him a bar lamp burst and dripped flaming oil from its wreckage. The other lamp dissolved and winked out an instant later.

In the flickering flare of the spilled oil he got a glimpse of Osterberg leading a charge at the doors and firing as they swung shut. On Osterberg's second shot, all guns together blared a prolonged explosion, until he shouted furiously, "Get out after 'em!"

In the lull a pair of guns outside spaced shots that ripped through the splintered doors and brought glassware cascading off the backbar shelves. Somebody said, "Bishop didn't get out, Owl!"

"I know damn well he didn't!"

"Ain't nobody getting out this minute!" Jay Nunn put in. "De Risa's covering the doors while his ladinos reload. We got to wait till they start off."

"Don't waste your time. Get Bishop!"

Bishop whirled and vaulted over the bar. One of Rico's haphazard bullets burned his arm. Landing on the bartender, he took a sprawl that gashed his hands on broken glass. The bartender let out an anguished gasp and dropped something that clattered on the floor.

He heard Kerry call out, "No!" So Rico had her, was preparing to pull out against her protests. This night was wrecking her trust in Rico.

The two guns ceased punishing the doors. Horse noises reached into the barroom. Don Ricardo called loudly, "Too bad, Rogue! Too damn bad." A note of actual regret tinged his voice. *"Adiós, amigo!"*

Hoofbeats fluttered down the road. The Hatchet men

promptly swarmed to the doors. A carbine roared and drove them back cursing. Don Ricardo had left a man behind to cover for a head start.

The spilled oil burned low. The cursing men stumbled about the overturned chairs. Osterberg shouted, "Get that Mexican out there! Get a light! Where the hell's Harry?"

A face bobbed up over the bar. "Harry? You there? Did Bishop—"

Bishop fired and the face dropped. With the gunbarrel he tapped the squirming bartender quiet and ran crouched along behind the bar.

A spot of faint light suddenly speared from the planking beside him and splinters stung his face. They knew he was behind the bar. Two or three more opened fire at it and other ragged little spots appeared.

He kept on along the bar until he reached the end, and paused under the flap to take quick stock. All he could see in the smoky darkness were the overturned chairs, some shifting figures, and here and there the snapping stab of a triggered gun. Then a match flared and he saw Eben Dekker hastily tipping the chimney of a window lamp.

A short way off, along to the left of the wall that blocked him, was the doorway to the cardroom. He measured the distance and judged the few seconds it would take Dekker to get the lamp lighted. As he made his stooping run he was thinking of Rico. Thinking that no chance was too long to take, to put a bullet in him.

Somebody spied his stooping figure, yelled, and got off a fast shot.

Bishop grunted "Hell!" and rolled the rest of the way. His left ribs felt sledge-hammered.

He pushed himself up on hands and knees and backed over the floor of the cardroom. Dekker got the lamp lighted and shadows came crowding up to the doorway. Bishop spent two shots, circled around a roulette layout, and squatted behind it, breathing hard.

"I got him with that one!" Colorado George said. "Look—blood on the floor. Hell, there's a trail of it behind the bar. Must be he's twice hit. How you feel, Bishop?"

"Fair," Bishop said and pitched a shot over the roulette layout. The brim of a hat spun back from the doorpost and a voice swore aggrievedly about a new Stetson ruined.

Osterberg said, "Only one Mexican left covering the front, ain't there? One lousy Mexican!"

"Yeah—and one lousy slug from that carbine can ruin you!"

"Draw his fire, and we'll rush him!"

"Aw, hell!" Colorado George sang out. "Let's get out the cardroom window an' pick him off, then go after de Risa!"

"How about Bishop in there?"

"A busted gunfighter!" Colorado George lunged in through the cardroom door, shooting blindly before him. He had a reputation for reckless impatience.

Bishop was wiping his hands on the floor, the blood from their cuts making them slippery, and he had to snatch up a gun and let fly on the instant. He sent Colorado George back out into the barroom dangling a useless arm, and somebody asked sardonically, "How busted is that gunfighter, George?"

Looking behind him he picked out the dim sheen of the window that Colorado George had spoken of, and he crawled backward to it, keeping the roulette layout between himself and the door. Pain stitched his side when he straightened up, but the fact that he could straighten up at all satisfied him that it wasn't the worst wound he'd ever received.

The shattered front doors of the barroom creaked. The carbine cracked from some distance off outside. A gun inside boomed twice. A squeal rose.

Osterberg cursed. "Hit his horse. He was pulling out."

"He ain't going nowhere now, not afoot," Jay Nunn said. "Jeez, Owl, we got to get after de Risa! He took her along. The boss won't like this!"

"There's a lot the boss don't like!"

Bishop tried the window of the cardroom. It slid up an inch, stuck there, and he had to lever it with a gunbarrel. It rasped badly as he pried it past the sticking point. He covered the sound of it with a fit of heavy coughing that made his ribs take fire.

"Cough it up, gunfighter!" Dekker jeered. "Got some more pills for you." He dashed across the doorway, firing in on the jump. Bishop spent a shot that sprayed splinters from the doorframe and must have tagged Dekker, for he heard him yelp.

He dragged himself over the sill of the window. It was a tight squeeze for him, and when halfway through he slid out headfirst onto hard earth. He got up and darted to the front corner of the saloon. To find a horse handy was more than he hoped for, yet there at the hitching rack stood his own horse, stamping nervously and tugging at its tied reins.

It shouldn't have surprised him, he guessed. It was typical

74

of Rico. Fix a man in a jackpot, but leave him his horse. Ironic punctillio. A mocking bit of tarnished code.

Lights had come on among the few buildings scattered about the crossroads. He saw the horse that Osterberg had shot; it lay dead on the south fork. And he saw Rico's man, the lone rearguard, a shadow furtively slipping through shadows, making for the horse at the hitching rack.

He moved out from the corner and motioned him off. The man brought up his carbine, needing that horse for his getaway, ready to kill for it. In mute threat Bishop lined a gun at him, but the man wasn't to be put off and as the carbine leveled steady Bishop shot him. The falling man jerked a discharge from the carbine that struck the road and whirred off. The horse danced.

Someone in the saloon bellowed, "Hell, there's two out there!"

Bishop freed the reins, swung up into the saddle, and lined the horse southward. With the hammering of his mount's hoofs came shouts and the noise of the Hatchet men stampeding to the saloon's doors. A gun barked. He hipped around in the saddle, shot two shots at the first of the murky figures swarming out of the saloon, and slapped the flank of the horse with the gunbarrel. The horse, a jughead that wasn't conditioned to fast starts, stumbled before settling to an even gait. Bishop grunted, the jolts sending fresh pain up his side.

When he looked back again, Forks was a cluster of lights in which men were running to wherever they had hidden their horses. There was no gunfire. They had discovered his absence from the cardroom.

The empty road before him bent to a sweep of rising hills bared of their trees and given over to grazing. The horse ran well, once it got stretched out. He strained his eyes to peer up forward to the distant skyline. Its rolling contour rose as a black barrier flat against the stars. One tiny segment of it rippled in movement. He watched the ripple pass on over the skyline. It was off the road, he judged. With only two men left and the Hatchet hunters after him, Rico would shun roads and travel the rough country.

"Heading for home all right," he said aloud. He thumbed fresh shells into the cylinders of his guns, a nimble task when riding, and tried to ignore his hurting ribs. "Damn woman-crazy sidewinder!"

NINE

The morning's sun greeted him with the overbright warmth of a cheerful idiot, increasing to dazzling heat as he pushed his drooping horse on through patches of chaparral interspersed with sand dunes. The glare of it, intensified by the reflected shimmer of the sand, smarted his eyes. He kept closing them, partly to shield them, partly from weariness.

His side ached like a bruise. It had stopped bleeding and his shirt had stuck to it. He tipped his hat forward and squinted ahead. Rico had angled westerly. A stiff breeze before dawn had drifted sand into the tracks and covered them, but there was no special reason to suppose that he had changed direction this morning. This southwest course probably meant he was making for Piedras Negras, somewhere around there.

"Got to make camp soon, or he'll be afoot," Bishop muttered. "Me too." He blew gathered dust from his lips, felt absently for his canteen, and remembered he didn't have one.

"Damn it," he said patiently.

He bent low to examine shallow indentations in sand that had been partly protected by thornbush from the dawn breeze. Hoofprints. He nodded. He was on the mark. Rico had forced the pace and kept going all through the night. Risked wearing out the horses. They hadn't been too fresh to begin with.

He sighed, coming out of the chaparral onto more eye-punishing, horse-crippling sand dunes. His short sigh turned to a grunt. Below the dunes, low down on the sharp horizon, a fringe of cottonwoods signified a stream. If the stream hadn't dried up too long ago, there ought to be grass. If there was water too, that would be Rico's camp for the day. He couldn't pass that up. Water, grass, and shade from the blazing sun.

He drew steadily closer to the cottonwoods. His horse, sniffing water, made an effort to hasten its shuffling gait. Rico would be there, unless he'd lost his mind.

Metal caught a brief glimpse from the sun. It puffed a wispy ball of smoke. The crack of the report sounded flat and tiny in the silence. Bishop listened to the thin whine of the bullet. A rifle, not a carbine. The bullet hit sand ahead of his horse. He looked down at the mark as he passed it and rode on.

Did Rico expect to turn him off with a warning shot? Did the warning arise from some odd scruple, like leaving his horse at the hitching rack? Bishop shook his head slightly, in no mood to figure out the vagaries of Rico's mind.

Two other glints appeared. He was within carbine range now and his thoughts went back to San Silvano. Rico had kept them from shooting at him there, but much had happened since then to destroy any semblance of friendship. Detachedly, he reckoned he didn't rate the courtesy of that warning shot.

Two figures, each a flamboyant spectacle in its own way, walked out from under the cottonwoods. Don Ricardo in his hard-worn charro elegance, Kerry Dyal in her dancehall finery. The leveled carbines remained motionless, braced against cottonwood trunks. The bone handles of Don Ricardo's guns winked little white flickers in rhythm with his footsteps as he walked, Kerry a step behind him.

Bishop rode up to them, pulled his horse to halt, and looked first to Kerry. She was shaking, dazed with fatigue, and what he read in her eyes was the faintest flicker of hope beneath full dismay. She was a very tired and disillusioned girl. Under pressure, her champion, the courtly Don Ricardo de Risa, had revealed his other side, that of the hard-bitten desperado.

He dismounted. Don Ricardo perceived the stiffness of that action. His rapid glance took in the haggard cast of Bishop's unshaven face, the reddened eyes, the compressed mouth. His glance dipped to the gashed hands, dried blood in the black creases and under the fingernails. Beneath the open coat, a blood-caked shirt.

"Rico," Bishop said tonelessly, "you lack guts."

Don Ricardo blinked twice, then his eyes grew intent and a shade speculative, as if he questioned Bishop's sanity.

"So? I would never say that about you, Rogue. You must be—"

"You lack guts," Bishop said again. "Osterberg was right where you're concerned. You were a ring-tailed scorcher once, but you're a busted gunfighter now. A has-been."

The intentness in Don Ricardo's eyes sharpened. His face clouded darkly without changing expression. "You believe that?"

77

"Last night I saw the evidence of it. You ran out on the Forks fight. You showed yellow."

"No! I got Kerry out of there. I told you if we—"

"I say you showed yellow!" Bishop flung at him. "You quit cold last night, and now you lack the guts to shoot it out with me."

Don Ricardo tapped febrile fingers against his thighs. "I'm ready when you are!" he breathed.

"Big talk," Bishop said. "Big talk from a has-been! Two carbines aimed at me ready to shoot me down as soon as I make a move! Walk back with me out of their range—both you and Kerry. The one of us that comes out alive takes her!"

Frowning, Don Ricardo slowly shook his head. "She goes to Mexico with me, not to Hatchet with you! I'll take no chances on that! It is her own choice. Ask her!"

Bishop turned to her. "Something I heard in the fight last night gave me more reason to think your father's not the one behind this thing," he told her. "They spoke of 'the boss'—and they didn't mean Osterberg, the range boss. If they'd meant your father they'd have called him 'the old man,' or maybe 'the big auger.' You know that. You're a Texan. Will you risk going back to Hatchet with me?"

"I—I don't know." She shook her head confusedly. "I'm so —so mixed up—"

"She is too tired out to think for herself," Don Ricardo stated. "We're all tired, in the saddle all night."

"So you pass up my offer," Bishop growled. "I wonder you didn't stay scraunched down in cover with your *orejanos* and bushwhack me, instead of sending that warning shot!"

A vein stood out and quivered on Don Ricardo's forehead. "That shot wasn't intended as a warning! I meant to shoot your horse. Somebody"—his glance touched Kerry—"happened to knock my rifle as I fired. I felt a little sad at leaving you in that Forks trap. It had to be done." He shrugged. "We agreed that we couldn't get along, so one of us had to go! Still, when I saw you riding up just now, damned if I wasn't glad you'd got out of it. That's why I aimed for your horse. To give you one last chance to get off my trail. One last chance. Now I'm changing my mind!"

"Why don't you tip a nod to those carbines, then?" Bishop let his eyes shine hard contempt. "Is it because you know I'll get off one shot before I drop? One will be enough. Enough to finish a yellow quitter!"

78

Don Ricardo's head jerked back, while his hands stilled. "You are pushing me, Rogue," he said very quietly.

"I'll push you further," said Bishop. He looked at the two pointing carbines, at the Don's hands, and flatly laid the rest of it on the line. "A job's got to be easy to suit you, or you won't stay with it. You don't have a whole gang of *orejanos* round to do the heavy lifting, and your sand's run out. The Hatchet setup got tough—so it's back to Mexico, tail between your legs! It adds up to yellow quitter, any damn way you look at it!"

Don Ricardo's face quivered, pale now. "You've gone too far!" He began a swift gesture with his left hand, halted it when Bishop's hand darted under his coat.

"Go on, Rico—finish it!" Bishop said. "Finish it, and we'll both go to hell together! Maybe that's your best bet. You'll still be a yellow quitter, but you won't have to live with it. In your boots, I think that'd be my choice."

Don Ricardo dropped his half-raised hand. He shuddered as though chilled, and moved his lips soundlessly before speaking.

"Me? Yellow? A quitter? *Me?*" The last of his self-control slipped. "I'll show you, Rogue Bishop!" he choked. "I'll show you how far I can go!"

Bishop barked a short dry laugh. "You were a good man once, Rico, but that day's gone. What happens to a good man when he turns yellow dog? You've seen it. So've I. He growls and yaps louder, trying to prove he's still a good man. But it takes more than yapping. There's always somebody who'll call his bluff. Then he's got to bite—or run!"

"I can bite!" the Don seemed to have difficulty in swallowing something. "I can bite as hard and fast as ever! I'll ride you a trail that'll break your nerve, Rogue Bishop! We'll go back. We'll go back to Hatchet and I'll take it! I have only three men left. Two here, and one—"

"The one you left behind tried for my horse and I had to shoot him. You're still yapping!"

Don Ricardo bared his teeth. "I'll take Hatchet and strip it blind! A has-been? If you're still around when I'm through with Hatchet, I'll make you eat that!"

"It's a bet," said Bishop, and his tired mind knew a moment of triumph.

Don Ricardo swung on his heels and stalked back to the cottonwoods, every movement betraying his fierce rage. Kerry Dyal stood undecided, looking first at one, then at the other. Her eyes fell on Bishop's blood-caked shirt. She opened her lips in silent woe for him. He took up the reins of his horse and he and she walked after Don Ricardo.

"Yeah, he can bite," he muttered to her. "He bit hard on that!"

She said in a small voice, "But you tried to force him into a fight with you!"

He nodded. "That was first choice. If it hadn't been that you're involved, he wouldn't have backed down. He wouldn't back down to anybody. Second choice was to make him turn back. It worked."

"It almost didn't! I thought he'd—"

"It was touch and go," Bishop admitted. "Now, about your father—"

"You really intend to take me back to him, don't you? In spite of everything?"

"Because of everything." He corrected her. "Yes, I do. And nothing's going to stop Rico from turning back now. He's got to prove he's no quitter. Got to prove it to himself, not just to me. What I did was open his eyes, show him the figure he cuts backing out of a scramble. Shook his tall opinion of himself—that's what makes him sore."

"You must know him very well."

"We've been through a few things together," he said sparely.

"And if you go through this, if you and he get through it alive," she said, "then you'll fight each other. You'll kill each other! Why? I mean, why go through with it? What can it gain you?"

He had lost sight of that for the time being, and having no ready reply he let a shrug do. Revolving it over in his mind, he concluded that it boiled down to a matter of first things first. Get her safely settled. After that, look to his own interests, if any. If none—well, hell, it was a sorry kind of man who wouldn't do his stint and forget the bill, once in a blue moon.

That was his answer to her question, but he left it unspoken because it wasn't entirely satisfactory and he suspected he'd fail to convince himself if he put it into words. It left out of account personal factors that he was disinclined to examine.

"You're a strange kind of man," Kerry said slowly. "I thought at first you were a—a gunman—"

"You weren't too far wrong. I'm a gambler, but on the side I call myself a troubleshooter. It's a gunfighting trade. I'm pretty much in a class with Rico, and you've seen now what he is." Bishop grinned faintly. "A lot of people are thinking the world would be a better place without the likes of him and me. Especially here in Texas!"

"Him, perhaps, but not you. May I call you Rogue?"

He didn't favor it, but his given name of Rogate lent itself to the nickname and he could never get rid of it. "Well, I've been calling you Kerry . . ."

They entered the fringe of cottonwoods. The stream ran a trickle and grass grew along the banks. Don Ricardo was talking in a mutter with his two men. Breaking the news to them, Bishop guessed, of the change in plans. Telling them, too, of what had happened to their *compadre* back at Forks. He took note of their bitter stares at him. Rico badly needed his help in any stab at Hatchet, but he would have it understood that the truce was hair-triggered.

Kerry followed Bishop down to the stream, and as he watered his horse she said, "I can't believe my father wants me back home alive and safe. I'd like to believe it—heaven knows I would—but I can't!"

"What I'm going to say might not please you," Bishop told her, "but here it is. You led a sheltered life, living with your mother. And a lonely year with your father. Your judgment of men is none too good. You think Frank Wittrock's your friend because he laid himself out to show you sympathy. I've learned enough about him to know he's not the pure Southern pilgrim he makes himself out to be. It surprised you how Osterberg and that crew of his acted to you at Forks. It didn't me. I knew what they are!"

"My father—" she began.

"You were wrong about Rico," he pursued. "You trusted him because of his pretty manners. Maybe he was born a blue-blooded *aristo*, as I've heard him sometimes claim. I doubt it. He's been a lobo ever since I've known him. Behind his bowing and scraping, he was laughing at you!"

"And you?" she demanded hotly, stunned by his brutal bluntness.

"I'm not laughing at you, nor didn't at any time. That's about the only difference. You asked to call me Rogue. It's short for Rogate, but that's not all. It was pinned on me because folks think it fits!"

He backed his horse from the water and led it onto grass. "What I'm leading up to is—you could be wrong about your father. I think you are."

"And you'd risk my life on your opinion!" she flashed.

"For your life I'm risking mine."

He regretted saying that as soon as it was out. To his own ears it smacked of the brand of florid heroics that Rico enjoyed indulging in at times.

On Kerry it had a far different effect. She hung her head and murmured, "That's true!" Then taking a quick breath and raising her face she said steadily, "Let me help you with your wound. It's the least I can do."

While Bishop was trying to decide how to meet her chastened mood without committing himself one way or another, Don Ricardo sang out curtly, "We will rest up the horses today and start back at sundown. Kerry, get some rest!"

Sundown, Bishop thought, was cutting it close. They'd reach Hatchet tonight on played-out horses, not a chance for a getaway if things blew up. The hard-used animals needed more than a day's rest, but Rico in his present mood was ready to ride a dying burro.

He peeled off his coat and knelt at the stream to soak loose his shirt. "Yeah, you get some rest," he told Kerry. "If we get to Hatchet you'll need to be fresher than you are now."

As an afterthought, he added, "We all will."

TEN

Bishop closed his hand over the nose of his horse, pinching off the beginning of an uneasy snort. One of Ricardo's men, Mateo, was coming back from night-scouting the Hatchet headquarters, slipping silently on foot with the effortless stealth of a born prowler.

Through the surrounding windbreaks of giant oaks no light was visible from the big house, nor from the long bunkhouse and outbuildings. Not even a night light in the yard.

Mateo passed Bishop without a word or sign, and went to Don Ricardo. They whispered together. The Don's tone sounded sharp. Eagerly querying. Mateo repeated something, shaking his head in positive denial.

"Well?" Bishop asked, and Don Ricardo moved over to confer with him.

"Nobody there," he said softly. By unspoken agreement they had shelved their feud and were working together. "Bunkhouse empty. Saddle racks empty too. Would they all be out at the roundup camps?"

"More likely out trying to cut our sign! Some, anyhow. Osterberg and the others."

"And nobody left here to guard the horse stock!"

"Still looking for an easy score, Rico?" Bishop murmured. "Sure, plenty of good Hatchet horses for the lifting. Plunder the house while you're at it. Might pick up a loose dollar or two."

Don Ricardo swore under his breath, eyes glinting. Like Bishop, he regarded himself as several cuts above the common run of badmen. Lifting a band of horses was one thing— a sporting proposition. To class him with a sneak thief was altogether else, a dangerous insult.

"Hell take your gringo tongue—!"

"And your Latin liver and lights!" Bishop grunted. "Now let's get on with it. Kerry, stay close by me."

She was already as close to him as could be without climbing into his pocket, and he rather wished she'd give him a little more room, but he wanted it understood whose orders she was to take.

"We won't want another bobble like last night in Forks," he told her, for Don Ricardo to hear. "Another run-out would strain my luck, such as it is."

He said no more on the subject, observing its perilous effect, and decided henceforth to let it drop. It had served its purpose. Rico, breathing hard through his nose, was close to the explosion point. He knew perfectly well that Rico hadn't pulled out of the Forks fight because of any loss of nerve, but it had made a useful barb while it lasted, one that he had pushed to the limit.

"Let's get on with it," he said again. "We'll settle our differences later."

"That we will!"

A final glare, and Don Ricardo motioned curtly to his two men. They had no set plan, for to try figuring ahead was useless. They had bent all their efforts toward reaching Hatchet without running afoul of Hatchet searchers and the law, and now that they had reached it misgivings came crowding. Bishop wondered if Rico saw it as he himself was suddenly seeing it. A foolhardy venture. Four hunted men and a girl advancing on Hatchet headquarters, no notion of what they'd find besides trouble, nor for that matter any definite idea of their purpose except somehow to secure the girl's rights. And even on that they were split. He couldn't recall ever getting himself into anything so hopelessly hairbrained as this.

They tied their horses under the oaks and stood for a moment gazing at the big house. Its tall uncurtained windows glimmered blankly back at them.

"Welcome home!" Don Ricardo murmured to Kerry.

His tone told Bishop that he wasn't alone in seeing the futile aspect of this thing. Rico had seen it clearly yesterday, sized it up as a fool's bet, and only the barbed taunts had blinded him to it. Now his astute sense was revealing it to him once more. But he would go into it with his eyes wide open. He wouldn't back out again, not while Bishop lived.

They paced on forward, entered the wide yard, paused a moment more to listen, and went quietly to the front door. Pushing open the door, Bishop felt Kerry trembling against him. She dreaded this barren, forbidding house. As a child she had known happiness in it, but all her associations with it these last years were unhappy, drab, or fearful.

"Brace up!" he muttered to her, and reluctantly she en-

84

tered with him. Starlight at the naked windows did little to relieve the darkness inside. They trod tiptoe on the bare floors.

"Like a damned morgue," Don Ricardo commented. He struck a match and irritably cursed one of his men. "Keep your thieving fingers off things, Chico! This is not a plunder raid."

"What is it, then?" Chico inquired reasonably. They were in the large room that was outfitted as the ranch office, Frank Wittrock's domain, and Chico promptly pilfered a box of cigars.

"It's an exploration," Bishop said. He took the box of cigars from him and replaced them on the desk, helping himself to a fistful.

Don Ricardo, striking a second match, snorted. "You spoke belittlingly to me of plundering the house!"

"A few smokes don't count." Bishop stuck one between his teeth and the rest in his pocket. "I was all out. Give me a light."

"The size of the theft is of no consequence," Don Ricardo said piously, holding out the match, "and necessity is not an excuse!"

"Have it your way."

"Thank you, I shall. You're a thief! You're also a hypocrite and—" He whipped out the match. "What is that?"

They stood motionless, listening to muffled sounds overhead. Somewhere a door opened and closed, and there came a steady *slap-slap* of slippers, the heavy and deliberate step of a man so familiar with his surroundings he didn't need a light in the dark.

"My father!" Kerry whispered. Her tone bore a mingling of dread and anticipation.

The approaching footsteps paused at the head of the staircase. "That you, Frank? What are you doing down there in the the dark?" Simon Dyal's strong, rough voice stirred echoes in the house. "Who's with you?" He sounded ill-humored.

Don Ricardo moved silently. Bishop's fingers closed over his wrist in a crushingly tight grip and forced his drawn gun back into its holster. In return Don Ricardo elbowed Bishop in his sore ribs and fetched a stifled grunt from him.

"Damn it, answer me! I heard you come in. Heard talk down there." The slippers slapped on the stairs, descending. Age hadn't dulled the old man's ears. Nor his nose. "I smell scent! You got a woman with you? Is that it?" He sniffed loudly. "Smells like a whorehouse!"

Kerry turned as if to run out and Bishop reached a long arm and restrained her.

Still receiving no reply, Simon Dyal bellowed, "What the hell's going on round here? Where've you been? Where's Osterberg and those sidekicks of his? Don't tell me they're out with the roundup crews, 'cause I know different! I'll fire 'em when I see 'em!" He paused. "Frank?"

They heard him smack the banister in his exasperation. "By God, I'll fire you too! Not worth a damn these last few days—never on hand when I want you! Now you come sneaking a woman into my house!"

As he reached the foot of the stairs he evidently made out their dark, unmoving figures, none resembling Frank Wittrock in outline.

"What the hell's this?" he demanded, suddenly cooling off, and padded briskly to the fireplace. Unerringly he located matches and a lamp on the mantel. A match scraped a light and he lit the lamp. Holding the lamp up he came forward.

He wore a shabby dressing town over an ankle-length nightshirt, and in his carpet slippers he was no taller than Kerry, but being a Texas cattleman he had automatically slapped on his hat before coming downstairs. Bishop had a little trouble remembering him as a forceful old tyrant who had given him the rough side of his tongue. He looked more comic than formidable, and at the same time pathetic, a bantam rooster without spurs. His face was the same, ugly, brown-stained and scarred, the mouth belligerent with its sideways twist and thick lower lip, the blooshot right eye sinisterly half shut, but the nightshirt and carpet slippers robbed him of toughness. The shabby dressing gown was quilted, a warm comfort for thin old blood on cool nights. The big hat made a clown of him.

"Rogue Bishop!" he snapped, as aggressive as ever, obviously not realizing his ludicrous appearance. "Who are these Mexicans?"

His tone displeased Don Ricardo, who drawled, "De Risa is my name. Put the lamp down before you drop it, old man."

"A pistolero and a couple of ladrones," Dyal commented. "You keep lousy company, Bishop!" Kerry's back was toward him and he glanced at her dress and asked, "Who's the scented-up female?"

She turned slowly. For a long moment they stared at each other. It was difficult to tell which was the more stunned by the other's extraordinary appearance.

Bishop guessed it likely that Kerry had only known her father in the dignity of full atire, stalking three inches taller in high-heeled boots, impressively masculine.

Dyal positively had never seen her rigged out as a dance-hall doxy. His face grayed over and the brown blotches took on a greenish shade. His bloodshot eye, wide open, flashed red. The upheld lamp shook in his hand.

"What have you done to her?" he ground hoarsely. "What have you done to my daughter?"

"Nothing's been done to her." Bishop took charge of the lamp before Dyal got an idea to throw it at him. He set it on the desk. "Those were the only decent clothes we could buy for her."

"Decent?" Dyal glared at the short red skirt. *"Decent?"*

"Well, maybe not, but they had to do. Her other things got left behind down in Mexico. We ran into several spots of trouble, and that was one of them. She wasn't kidnaped, Dyal. She was tricked into going away of her own accord."

Emotions fought in Dyal's face. His eyes never left Kerry.

"Her own accord?" he echoed incomprehensively. He took half a step toward her, and stopped as if too unaccustomed to showing sentiment and uncertain of her response.

"And," Bishop said, "she didn't want to come back!"

That got through to him. His belligerent mouth seemed to shrink. "Didn't want to—why, Kerry? Why?" He took another step toward her.

Don Ricardo spoke up. "Old man, you're either a fool or a mad scoundrel! I was engaged to escort her secretly from here and do away with her, the ransom to be my payment! By your orders!"

"No!"

"Yes!" Don Ricardo said cruelly. "The money was yours. If not your orders, then whose? You hate your daughter! You wanted her killed!"

"Wait, Rico," Bishop cut in. "Dyal, your son sent her a letter. As she can tell you when she finds her voice, he warned her that you murdered her mother and planned to murder her too!"

"Good God!" Dyal burst out. "You believed that, Kerry?"

"Why not?" Bishop demanded. "She already suspected her mother was murdered. So do I. She had to move back in here, and what kind of a life did you give her? You call this miser-able damn place a home for a girl? No other women around,

87

nobody to talk to, and her father a sour old vinegaroon who wouldn't give her a kind word if she lay dying!"

His censorious blast, coming after Don Ricardo's accusation and Kerry's condemning silence, completed the break-up of Simon Dyal.

"Oh, my God!" He pressed a hand to his eyes, shutting out the sight of their stony faces. "My own child! Anne's child! Our Kerry-girl!"

"Your own flesh and blood," Bishop concurred. "And you treated her like a stranger. Worse. Like an unwanted stray. Shut her out of your life. Made her afraid of you. De Risa's the one who took her away from here, and I'm the one who's mostly responsible for bringing her back. Damned if I know which of us ought to be shot!"

They, the trespassers, in abrupt reversal became the accusers. Mateo and Chico, too, wore expressions of contempt. The most beggarly peon sheltered his children, gave them affection. The Hatchet owner stood as the defendant.

He dropped his hands and looked at them, and said in a wavering voice, "But you're wrong—wrong! Hate her? No, no!" None of the rough force remained to him. He was a little old man stammeringly protesting a monstrous charge.

"Her mother—I loved Anne so much I—" He made a futile gesture. "You don't know. Nobody knows. I love our daughter. It's just that I couldn't seem to—couldn't talk with her. Like a wall. A mile wide. Like strangers. Both of us strangers. Both." He swallowed painfully and whispered, "God knows I love my Kerry-girl!"

Kerry ran to him. There was a second's hesitation as they met, and in that instant Bishop saw Kerry's face so glowingly alive that it startled him. She threw her arms around her father, protectingly, as if she were the stronger one, shielding his ludicrous appearance from the disrespectful view of outsiders.

Bishop turned his back. He found himself listening for the sound of her laughter, but she was crying quietly, and he stared at Don Ricardo.

"That's how it is, Rico."

Don Ricardo gazed on unabashed. He too had glimpsed the bright change in Kerry's face. "Touching," he murmured, his eyes deliberately cynical. "Very touching. Damned if the old man isn't shedding some tears, too. Puts a lump in your throat, doesn't it?"

He swung on his heel, paced the length of the room, paused

to cock his head appreciatively at Kerry's painted portrait, and came on back.

"Must hurry," he said, "before Osterberg's guns come rounding in. A bit awkward, this heartwarming reunion. And the old man—you said he was tough. A tough old rawhide, you said."

"That's what he is, when he's fixed for it."

"A front, eh? Old burro in a lion's skin! Not a good kick left in him. She sees that now. Fond daughter and aging parent, damn it! Makes a difference."

Bishop gazed at him over the lighted lamp on the desk. "It does, Rico, it sure does!"

Don Ricardo threw his head up. His musing eyes hardened. "Not that much difference! You know what I set out to do, Rogue Bishop. I made it plain. He dies, she inherits!"

"And—"

"She can sell it—from Mexico, where she is going with me!"

'We've got something to settle between us before then."

"I haven't forgotten it!"

Don Ricardo set his mouth tight and straight. "He hasn't many years ahead of him in any case. Mateo and Chico take a sensible attitude toward death in such circumstances. Would I go soft because of an old man? One old man between me and"—he glanced at Kerry—"the prize of my life?"

Kerry, overhearing his words, stared at him in horror. A rush of color to Simon Dyal's face indicated that he also had heard. His mouth regained its belligerence. He ran a coolly estimating look at the desk.

"No, Rico." Bishop shook his head, stepping back from the lamp. "No, you won't go soft. Once, I'd have bet odds—on you'd give any man an even break—you could afford to, and you had pride. Not now. Yeah, you'd murder him for his daughter and his property. *But you won't!*"

His hands hit *slap-slap* in the swiftest double cross-draw of his life, no warning, so hard that the cuts reopened and blood filled them.

"You won't!" he said again.

Don Ricardo had snapped into movement at the first flick of the draw. His right hand struck, started up with its compact load. He halted it, staring stonily into the black muzzle wickedly aimed at his face. Mateo and Chico, Bishop's left-hand gun on them, remained motionless and taut—dark statues, only their eyes were alive.

Simon Dyal put Kerry from him and stepped in front of her.

His face revealed nothing but a cold weighing of events. He looked years younger, strong and masterful, not ludicrous.

For a long moment Don Ricardo studied the gun in his face. He had seen Bishop's guns often, though not from that angle. He was figuring what chance he had of completing his draw. The chance didn't exist. He abandoned the figuring and sought another approach.

"What now, Rogue Bishop?" His eyes glanced dartingly all about for inspiration.

"I think I'll have to kill you, Rico."

Bishop uttered the statement simply, without heat. He too had followed the code that demanded of a gunfighter that he give any man an even break. Without it, a gunfighter lost his right to pride, fell to the rank of common gunman. He hadn't given Rico an even break, making his draw. He wished that he could call up a hard rage, to squeeze the trigger and be done with it.

"I think I'll have to," he repeated. "Damn you for making me do it. Damn you to hell, Rico!" The rage wouldn't rise. For too many years, dispassionate efficiency had ruled the ultimate act of gunpoint violence. He had to do this in cold blood.

"Behind you!" Don Ricardo whispered urgently. "Behind you, Rogue—!"

"It's no use, that tired old trick."

"The windows—!"

"You'd pull that on *me?*"

"*Sangre de dios,* will you look—"

Owl Osterberg's voice cut across the whisper. "Don't move! Drop the guns, Bishop, that's all!"

Slowly, Bishop half-turned his head, the hard rage at last pounding up in him—rage at himself, and at Rico for distracting all of his vigilance this one minute.

Osterberg held a cocked gun steady on the sill of an open front window. He was crouched, his staring round eyes reflecting the lamplight like glass marbles. Close behind him stood Jay Nunn, Eben Dekker with a bandaged neck, and Colorado George, his arm in a sling. Each held a gun sighted.

"Never mind Bishop," Simon Dyal told them. "He's doing right."

They ignored him.

"Drop 'em!" Osterberg said. "Drop 'em right now!"

Bishop ran a look over the other tall windows. They were closed, and the lamplight shone on the uncurtained panes,

90

but muzzles caught gleams and he made out blurred faces above them.

"Shoot him, Owl!" Colorado George urged. "Goddam him, I will!"

"You mess this up, I'll bust your other arm! Bishop—!"

Bishop sighed, opening his hands, letting his guns tumble to the floor. He shook his head at Don Ricardo, who hissed Spanish oaths while his curved hands edged toward his holsters.

"You've got us killed, Rogue!"

"We'll all be dead if you draw!"

Simon Dyal spoke again, in his old sharp manner. "Osterberg! Never mind Bishop, you hear me? Let him pick up his guns!"

Disregarding his order, the range boss said over his shoulder, "Keep 'em covered tight while I go in."

He entered by the front door. Carefully circling the room, he came up behind Don Ricardo, plucked his pair of guns from their holsters, and tossed them along the floor to the front. The Don stiffened angrily at the disrespectful handling of his fine six-shooters. Osterberg kicked Bishop's guns after them, then stripped Mateo and Chico of their carbines, pistols, knives.

"Gather 'em up, Jay!"

Jay Nunn came in and gathered up the weapons, carrying them outside. He didn't look at Simon Dyal nor Kerry.

"How'd you know we were here, Owl?" Bishop inquired conversationally.

"We didn't." Osterberg went around opening the windows from the inside. "Figured you'd quit the country, making for Mexico. Hadn't been we needed a change of horses before takin' up your trail—" he shrugged. "George turned for home ahead of us, 'count of his arm. Saw your horses under the oaks and dropped back to tell us."

"That's why we didn't hear you ride in."

"We Injun'd in on foot. You mighta heard us at that, only you was busy stickin' a gun in de Risa's mustache and he was busy swallerin' cotton."

Simon Dyal was scowling in wrathful perplexity. "Who gave you leave to take hands off work and go chasing round the country?" he demanded. "I told Frank Wittrock to hire San Antonio detectives for that job."

Osterberg took notice of him for the first time. "Did you, now? I reckon he forgot."

"Who're those other men out there?"

"Nobody you know."

"Who *are* they?"

"Well, Frank and me hired 'em, but they sure as hell ain't no detectives!" The remark brought a rumble of laughter from the men at the windows. Without a trace of humor, Osterberg added, "On the payroll they're extra hands."

"We don't need extra hands on Hatchet! The roundup crews are full!"

"Who said they ain't?"

The insolence of the range boss, on top of his disregard of orders, snapped Dyal's already strained temper. His ugly old face darkened, and when he found his voice it came out bawling.

"Draw your time and get off Hatchet! Take those men with you—your three pals too!"

Osterberg's face twitched in what was for him the nearest thing to a smile. "That'll be the day!"

"What?" Dyal's bellow rang through the house. "Where's Frank Wittrock? By God, I warned him he favored the wrong man! He'll do no more hiring round here. Where is he?"

"I'm not on the moon, so lower your voice," Frank Wittrock drawled, entering. "In fact, shut up! Owl, bat him down if he sounds off again like that!"

ELEVEN

Simon Dyal opened his mouth to utter a roar of outrage, and wisely checked it when Owl Osterberg raised a threatening fist.

"Have you all gone crazy?" he asked in a forcedly moderate tone. "What d'you think you're doing, Wittrock—taking Hatchet over? Those grabbing days are dead'n gone. Here in Texas, anyway. Title deeds and lease contracts, registered brands, bills of sale and conveyance . . . It's all got to be legal nowadays, signed and sealed. You *must* be crazy!"

Don Ricardo met Bishop's glance, and murmured, "What are they after, making so bold with him? The old man knows what he's talking about. They couldn't lift a Hatchet calf, unless they carried it off to Mexico. And the market there for wet cattle is not so good."

Bishop nodded. "You ought to know." He watched Frank Wittrock pull the swivel chair out from the desk and seat himself in it.

"This is a queer affair!"

"It's wrong as hell, yeah."

"You let us in for it, damn you! What the devil are they going to—"

"I guess we're about to find out." Bishop shot a look at Kerry. What she and her father were about to learn, he feared was that they had come to understand each other too late. Recalling how he had asked her to trust him, he winced. Rico on his own might have done a better job: *Dyal dies, she inherits, and if Dyal's son turns up to claim anything, take care of him too!* Starkly simple plan.

Frank Wittrock swung the chair around so that he sat confronting Dyal, and after hitching up the knees of his pants he crossed his legs. He looked every inch a gentleman—light gray suit, white linen shirt, and silk cravat. He wore straight-heeled riding boots, English style, which Bishop noted were dusty, and a broad-brimmed planter's hat. No gun visible.

He took off his hat and laid it behind him on the desk, and using both hands he smoothed back his fair hair. The act had about it a studied affectation, like a mannerism adopted to prolong the moment before he replied to Dyal's question. He followed it by inspecting his fingernails. The men began shifting restlessly.

Dyal said, "You heard what I asked you! What're you up to?"

Frank Wittrock raised his light eyes. "I'm finishing what I started. It's three years since I came here to keep your books for you. Every day of those three years—every hour —I've looked forward to this. Lord, how I looked forward to it!"

He spoke so softly that his voice couldn't reach to the men at the windows. Osterberg and Jay Nunn stepped closer to listen. He motioned them off, saying, "You know enough. You don't have to know it all. Take those two Mexicans out."

"What you want done with 'em?"

He sent Osterberg an impatient look. "You have to ask? Leave Bishop and de Risa here—there'll be a use for them."

Osterberg jerked a thumb at Mateo and Chico, and they tramped out, their faces woodenly fatalistic.

"That's murder, Owl," Bishop said, seeing the range boss cock the hammer of his gun. He laid a narrow look on Wittrock's pale face and eyes, searching him for weakness. "This isn't the Square Deal Bar in Laredo!" he said, hoping for a reaction.

Wittrock gazed at him without any expression of startlement. "How was Dee when you saw her?" he asked unconcernedly, and Bishop realized that the five trackers had reported to him.

"She was bitter."

"I'm not surprised."

Two shots exploded outside and there was the unmistakable sound of two falling bodies. Don Ricardo bit his lip. His fingers played a futile game with his empty holsters.

"That's murder," Bishop said again. He looked toward the men at the open windows to calculate how they took it. Their faces reflected hard indifference. Gunmen. Their kind would shoot a Mexican on a bet to see which way he'd fall, an Indian for sport, and a white man for fifty dollars.

Frank Wittrock said to Dyal barely above a whisper, "I'm good at figures. Should be—I've worked in a bank, among other things. Damn little I knew of cattle ranching, but I learned, and when you recognized my sterling qualities you made me your business manager. It pleased your importance to have

94

a Southern gentleman at your beck and call, didn't it? Simply to hang onto me, you gave me more and more responsibilities."

"Nothing of the kind!" Dyal retorted. "I've never liked your fancy airs, but you showed you had a good head for business. You seemed able to handle men, too, so I let you take on some of that end. I see now I gave you too much rope!" He shook his head angrily. "What're you driving at? If you're out to rob me, cut the cackle and say so!"

"I'm having my say in my own good time. I'll not spoil this by rushing it." Wittrock gazed fixedly at him. "I've hated you all my life!"

Dyal stared back blankly. "You've only known me these three years."

"All my life! By name."

"What call have you got to hate me? I've made a few enemies in my time, but I don't recall any Southern gentleman among 'em."

Wittrock perked his colorless lips. "I'll tell you what kind of Southern gentleman I am. In my boyhood I was a New Orleans street rat. I begged, stole, pimped, rolled drunks—I killed a man before I was twelve. My stepfather. He was a drunken bum, and I knifed him for beating my mother. She was an available lady of the night, if you gather my meaning." His glance played over Kerry's dress, and Kerry, her eyes wide, shrank closer to her father.

"A bogus Southern gentleman and a born crook!" Dyal commented. "What's it got to do with hating me?"

"As I grew older," Wittrock went on, "I worked in the gambling houses. It was from the wealthy sports that I began picking up the right kind of manners and speech." He smiled reminiscently. "That came easy. My mother had learned the same way. With some fast manipulation I turned some tricks, till a house spotter caught on and they beat hell out of me. Took me months to walk again."

Don Ricardo, listening, sent Bishop a baffled look. "Why does he tell this?"

Wittrock heard the murmur, and said, nodding at Dyal, "He asked why I hate him, and I want him to know. Before he dies I want him to know the kind of life I've lived and what I've done since coming here!"

His whispery voice dripped venom. A spasm pinched his face to a pale mask of cruel resentment. He breathed deeply several times, gradually restoring his attitude of cool self-possession, and went through an elegant act of languidly stroking his chin, little finger extended.

"The gambling houses blackballed me. I'd risk another beating if I showed my face in any of them. Through a young fool of my acquaintance I got a job in his father's bank. I had something on him that his father didn't know about. Naturally, I turned my talents to best account—cooked my books and got away with a bundle of the bank's cash. That was when I came to Texas and changed my name."

"A born crook!" Dyal repeated. He worked his lips as if to spit out a bad taste in his mouth. "Thief, pimp, blackmailer, bank absconder—! By God, you sound proud of yourself!"

Wittrock let his eyes glint cold humor. "And murderer!" he said softly.

"Yes, that too! Killed your stepfather."

"Oh, I don't count that as a murder. Just a killing to protect my mother from a worthless drunk. She covered up for me. Drug his body off down an alley and let the Johnny Laws find him. She'd have killed him herself if she could."

"So that wasn't your only killing, eh?"

Shaking his head, Wittrock said, "Not by a long shot! Only my first. The one I meant was your wife. The fire she died in wasn't any accident. I set it!"

The next instant he held a stubby derringer in his hand, and was rising fast out of the swivel chair, for Dyal lunged at him. The threat of the pistol wasn't going to stop Dyal, and Bishop grabbed hold of him.

"Goddam, let me go!" Dyal struggled madly. "Let me at him!"

Bishop tightened his arms in a better grasp. A quick look at Kerry showed her to be standing frozen, her face numb from shock. There'd be no trouble from her for the moment. He said to Dyal, "Do I have to knock you out? That sneak gun could tear your leg off!"

"It certainly could," Wittrock agreed, wagging it. It was a two-shot Philadelphia .50 caliber, a fearsome weapon up to five paces. "That's just where I'd shoot him, so hang onto him. He's not going to die before he hears the rest, not if I can help it."

Reseating himself, he again performed the pants-plucking and crossed his legs. The derringer he held at rest on his knee.

"I hoped to get both of them in the fire—your wife and daughter. Kerry got out, unfortunately, so I had to make

96

other plans for her. It took time, a whole year to put her in the frame of mind to quit Hatchet. Osterberg—I knew him down in Laredo years ago—picked de Risa for the job. A mistake. De Risa crossed us up."

He looked at Don Ricardo, and yawned, covering the yawn delicately with two fingers.

"You're going to pay hard for that, you double-crossing Mexican dog!"

"I expect to, you white-eyed gringo mongrel!" responded Don Ricardo. He watched the snub snout of the derringer come to bear on him. "What is the rest of your entertaining little story? I am curious to know how you plan to profit from such peccadilloes."

Wittrock held the derringer steady for a moment longer, lowered it, and spoke to Dyal. "Remember the letter you received from your long-lost son? The letter that split up you and your wife? The letter than informed you that your first wife was still alive? I wrote it."

Dyal had ceased struggling in Bishop's grip. A dawning comprehension came into his face. He growled, "Why, you murdering swine!"

"In actual fact," Wittrock said, "your first wife died twenty years ago. That was the year before you married Anne Addison. I checked into the records when I began tracing you. Isobel LeBaron was the name of your first wife. She was my mother."

"My son—you?" Not the slightest sign of sentiment touched Dyal's grim face. "You're Trevor? How could I spawn such a critter! Must be you take after her."

Wittrock's light eyes sparkled like ice. A white ring appeared around his mouth. The derringer rose. "Don't you dare speak a word against her to me! You abused her and drove her out! Forced her to run off with that newspaper tramp!"

"That's a lie!" Dyal said heavily. "She picked up and left me, after shaming me with her goings-on. I didn't have money then, and she thought he did."

"Don't you say more like that! I'll smash you! She never lied to me! How many times she told me, when things got bad and we were broke, how it came we were what we were —outcasts! She taught me to hate you for driving her out, you—!"

"She hated herself for botching up her life, I reckon, and

97

wouldn't admit it to you. She always had to blame somebody else for her own—"

"Because of you she was forced to make her living from men! Sports!" Wittrock's raging whisper went on. "Lost her looks and sank lower and lower—and in New Orleans a woman can fall a long way down! Died of disease, buried in a pauper's grave!"

"I'm sorry to know that. But she—"

"You're sorry? *Sorry?* Because of you I was a street rat, clouted and kicked by the Johnny Laws, grand folks holding their noses from my stink! Raiding garbage in winter when the foodshops shuttered up their fronts! Shivering in my rags all night in doorways and stables—even the horses despised me! They used to curl their lips and nip at me. A thousand times I swore you'd pay for it all if I ever found you! A million times!"

"If I'd known you were alive and where you were, I'd have come and got you," Dyal said.

"And I'd have knifed you for what you did to my mother!"

"I tell you she brought it on herself. If you asked some of the old-timers round San Antonio—"

"I know all the lies you spread about her!"

Words were useless in the face of Wittrock's passionate conviction. His life-long hatred blinded him to all reason. Remembering the garrulous pair of old-timers in the Irishman's livery stable and their salty comments about the actressy woman Simon Dyal had rashly married in his youth, Bishop thought it likely that Dyal had considered himself well rid of her; but that didn't mean he had driven her out. He wondered if Dyal had questioned in his mind the paternity of the woman's infant son, and if he questioned it now with more doubts than ever. There certainly existed no family resemblance whatever between them, not one single trait or feature.

"I'm going to own Hatchet and every dollar you've got!" Wittrock said. "I'm your son and—"

"So you say!"

"What do you mean by that?" The derringer pointed dangerously at Dyal's middle. "It's on the records in San Antonio. I have proof of my identity. If there's any question about it, I can get more proof from New Oreleans—a pile of it. I'm your son and heir!"

Dyal eyed him with stark loathing. "Not on your scummy life! I made my will last year, leaving everything to Kerry, and sent it to my lawyer. In case of her death before mine, everything goes to my wife's Kentucky cousins."

"I know. It was with some letters I took to mail." Wittrock smiled thinly. "I destroyed it. You'll die intestate, as the lawyers say, and the courts will award your estate to your only living descendant—your long-lost son. Me."

He leaned back in the swivel chair.

"And that," he ended, "is what I set out to do."

TWELVE

Simon Dyal took Kerry's hand. Full understanding of Wittrock's intention flooded their faces and struck them voiceless. What they showed was incredulity rather than fear, an aghast disbelief of a purpose so inhumanly evil.

Bishop, keeping an eye on the derringer, said, "You haven't done it yet. You're a long way from it."

"Long? How long is a minute?" Wittrock slipped out a gold watch from his vest pocket and snapped open the case. "It won't take that long to shoot the four of you!"

"That the watch your mother gave you?"

Wittrock raised surprised eyes. "How did you know?"

"Dee Hazard mentioned it."

"She talked too much to you, the bitch!"

" 'To Trevor with love from Mother.' It didn't mean much then. It did later, though I couldn't be sure. Not a common name."

"You're talking to make time, aren't you, Bishop? A few more seconds won't help you." Wittrock drew out a clean white handkerchief and painstakingly wiped the face of the gold watch. "It's very fitting to use this on this occasion."

"It would seem so to you," Bishop said.

He could see how it would. The watch was a cherished keepsake from the only person Wittrock probably had ever had any feeling for, his mother. She must have bought it for him during a flush spell, and he must have hung onto it through many hard periods in his life. There had been a strong attachment between them, the stronger because they were two outcasts against the world, and in his warped obsession Wittrock was avenging her downfall and death.

"I don't need to make time," Bishop belied. "Sure, you can shoot me. You can shoot de Risa. The law wouldn't press too many questions about it. We're both posted, and we've run our score up these past few days."

Osterberg, at the door, intoned countingly, "San Antonio —Laredo—Carrizo Springs—Bandera—Forks. You sure have!"

100

Bishop went on speaking to Wittrock in a tone of mild argument. "You might shoot Dyal and get away with it, if you can make it look right, I don't know. He's a big man hereabouts. Solid citizen. Call it a toss-up chance. I'd bet even money either way. But murder a girl, here in Texas? *Hoo-wee!*"

"He's right," Don Ricardo chimed promptly. "He's all wrong with me, but he's dead right on that. Frame it any way you will—make it appear an accident—use every precaution—it will catch up with you! Nobody kills a good girl in Texas and goes free! Nobody!"

"A good girl?" Wittrock gestured at Kerry with the derringer. "In that get-up? It'll be plain to anybody she came back a tough little Lulu from Mexico, with cattle thieves and gunmen! Came back with them to rob her father, and got shot in the dark!"

"I suppose you trust these men of yours now, because they're on the payroll. But later on, when they drift away?" Don Ricardo began to sweat. "Won't they talk? A few drinks some night—loose tongues—the law! It is bound to leak out that you murdered her, no matter what you do! You can't stop talk!"

"Who'd talk?" The query came from Osterberg, pacing forward from the doorway.

"You wouldn't, Owl," Bishop granted, taking it up from Don Ricardo who was running out of words. "You're a wise one. You'd keep your mouth shut and take your pay. It'd be high pay for guaranteed silence. I know you!"

He saw Wittrock's eyes sharpen. He had uncovered a future eventuality that Wittrock had overlooked in his intense concentration on the present moment. Blackmail. Rico had already shaken his confidence that he could safely murder Kerry.

"Osterberg," Wittrock said. His eyes searched narrowly the frowning face of the range boss. "Take them out, the four of them. You and Nunn, Dekker, George. Divide them among you as you like, but make it look—"

He stopped speaking.

Osterberg was slowly shaking his head. Behind him at the open door, Nunn, Dekker, and Colorado George edged back as if suddenly shy of the lamplight.

"Not me, Frank," Osterberg said. "I'll take out Bishop and de Risa, sure. A pleasure. The old man—uh-uh. The girl—*uhn-uhn!* You're asking too much. Put my neck in a noose?"

"You weren't backward about hiring de Risa to do it! And last night in Forks—"

"That was diff'rent, hiring de Risa, no backfire on me. Nobody took any shot at her in Forks or any other place I know of. You wanted her, we tried to catch her for you."

"A thousand dollars? Two thousand?"

"Not for ten thousand! A girl? Simon Dyal's daughter? If I didn't hang for it I'd use up the rest o' my life running!"

"Nunn?" Wittrock snapped. "Dekker? George?"

Nunn merely shook his head. Dekker said, "A man wouldn't live long enough to spend the money." Colorado George said, "You couldn't even pay me to see it!"

One of the men at the windows inquired, "What's going on, a raffle? The young lady looks tired—they oughta let her sit."

"There you are!" Don Ricardo folded his arms, in his eyes a vast relief and a rising gleam of craftiness that caused Bishop a twinge of foreboding. "You can't hire anybody to do it for money. Your gunmen draw the line at what you want done. They have some scruples left. Not Osterberg—he'd do anything, like you. But he values his neck too much to invite the hangman!"

"And if you've got any sense," Bishop put in, "you won't do it yourself!"

He considered that he and Rico between them had gone far toward pressing home their point. Their own lives could be written off, and Simon Dyal's life hung by a hair, but a chance remained of saving Kerry's life and that was as much as they could hope to salvage. Still, he didn't like the look in Rico's eyes.

Wittrock fingered the derringer, staring at Dyal and Kerry, the unforeseen problem creasing his brow. "There has to be a way," he breathed. "There must be! Thought I had it— accident—shots in the dark . . . That won't do." He was cogitating, whispering his thoughts. "I'll figure it out. Got to!"

"What you need," Don Ricardo drawled with sinisterly helpful insinuation, "is a goat! Know what I mean? Somebody to take the blame. A guilty culprit for the law to hunt."

The light eyes slid to him. "How's that?"

"For this," Don Ricardo enlarged, "you want a man who is so badly out of law that it doesn't matter to him what more he does. A man so desperate he'll stop at nothing. Pick a badly wanted outlaw, one who is in a desperate fix—and

102

there's your goat! I am surprised you haven't thought of it, a man of your intelligence."

The sly suggestion, and the compliment, took effect. Wittrock, his face clearing, said to Osterberg, "Go on outside. Pull the men back a bit, but keep watch."

He waited while Osterberg walked out, waited until the men outside drew back from the windows at Osterberg's muttered command, before speaking to Bishop and Don Ricardo.

"Which one?"

Don Ricardo scowled. "The idea came from me!"

"It makes no difference to me which of you does it." Wittrock reached behind him to the desk drawer. He opened the drawer and extracted a gun from it. The faintly lingering hope in Dyal's eyes died. "Your gun," Wittrock said to him, punching out its shells. He placed the emptied gun and three of the shells, loose, back in the drawer. "Well?"

"What do you offer?" Don Ricardo asked.

"A fresh horse and a good long start."

"Promises come cheap," Bishop said to Don Ricardo.

"Not that promise!" The Don eyed Wittrock steadily, smiling. "That goat must have his getaway! Alive and on the run, he carries the guilt with him, eh, Wittrock? Dead, he is a danger. To kill him here would look too neat, a smell of frame-up about it. The law would ask suspicious questions and poke around here until something came to light. No, no, the law must go hunting after him, sure of his guilt, your men truthfully swearing to it! But you see that, Wittrock, I'm sure."

Wittrock returned his gaze meditatively. "I see it. The horse will be brought up to the back of the house. I'll be there. And Osterberg. We'll shoot in the air. Are you the one?"

"Who better qualifies? If I can get there, I'll go back to Mexico and never again set foot in Texas. You won't ever need to fear I'll talk! Besides, I'm the man Osterberg chose to take the girl from here and do away with her. Doesn't that give me first right? You can't trust Bishop!"

"Nor you! You crossed us up on that!"

Don Ricardo coughed. "I take this opportunity to show my integrity, then, and suggest that you have a story ready to cover the event," he said airily. "It will come out, of course, that I took the girl for ransom. Very well, I brought her back, but my accomplice, Bishop, demanded more ransom, and—oh, you can make up a convincing story! Let me have the gun."

"When I'm gone, slip it out of the desk and load it with your back turned." Wittrock got up and moved away. "When you've fired the three shells, bring it out back and drop it before you get on the horse. After that you're clear. Any bad move, you're dead! Just one mistake!"

"I rarely make mistakes.

"They'll be watching you—Nunn, Dekker, George—"

"Witnesses." Don Ricardo nodded. "Witnesses to swear they saw me do it. You're a wise man."

Bishop moved a step over to Dyal and Kerry, and heard the old man's heavy breathing. He laid his hand on Kerry's shoulder. She looked up into his face, but he was watching Don Ricardo shift casually to the desk and lower the wick of the lamp.

As he paced on outdoors, Wittrock announced, "This is for the county sheriff to take over. Anybody know where he'd be?"

Somebody answered, "Forks, maybe, looking into last night's bust-up. Want me to ride down?"

"Never mind."

Wittrock spoke again in a lowered voice and they heard him tread on around the house, while another pair of footsteps hurried toward the corrals. Nunn, Dekker, and Colorado George loomed up at one of the open windows, peering in.

"What's wrong with that lamp?" Nunn asked.

"Wick needs trimming." Don Ricardo turned it up high and it flared yellow, sending up smoke and streaking the glass chimney black. He turned it down low again.

Back turned to them, he slid open the drawer and his hands worked swiftly at loading the three shells into the gun. They weren't supposed to know what he was doing, but their wary eyes told that they knew he was carrying out his instructions from Wittrock. The other men, farther out, were lighting up cigarettes here and there, and falling into quiet talk.

"Your turn, Rico," Bishop murmured to him. "Your trick. It's all yours."

"All mine." Holding the gun hung flat before him, he stole a glance over his shoulder. The small action caused the three men at the window to stiffen. Nunn had got a rifle and he raised it.

"Yes, my trick." Don Ricardo brought his face forward. He was not smiling, looking first at Kerry, then at Bishop. "I wonder if you would do what I'm going to do?"

"I don't want to live that much!"

104

"I think you would." He bent his head to look down at the gun. "I don't know if you could. You called me yellow, a quitter. Why you did, I know now, and I pass it off. But you also called me a has-been, and that still stings. I am going to prove you a liar!"

He fell silent, his head bent then in an attitude of listening. Presently, there came the muffled footfalls of a horse being led up to the back of the house. He waited another minute. A dry cough sounded, and he quirked his lips.

"Friend Wittrock is impatient! I must do this quickly!"

He lowered his voice to a whisper. "I am going to shoot fast, one-two-three. You first, Rogue. You next, Dyal. Then you, Kerry. Fall hard in your turn, and make it look real—because I shall miss all three of you! Ready, Rogue!"

The gun roared. The blast of it across the lamp whipped the flame to a smoky flicker. Bishop contracted his face muscles, let his body go limp, and before his knees thumped the floor, Don Ricardo fired again. For an instant it seemed that Dyal had failed to understand, had let his turn pass; then he pitched headlong forward. The third shot brought Kerry crumpling down.

In the stunned silence, Don Ricardo's whisper barely reached Bishop's ears.

"It's yours now, Rogue!"

The lamp went out. His footsteps sped through the house, while the men out front raised startled yells. A door at the rear banged open.

"Why the hell did you put out the lamp?" Wittrock's voice snapped.

"In case of accidents—Nunn's rifle, for instance! Where's Owl?"

"Right here, Mexican! Throw down the gun and get goin' before this goes off in your back! Watch out for him, Frank, he's Injun-wild after killin' the three!"

Hoofs stamped the hastening patter of a horse getting underway from standstill. Gunshots burst after it. The hoofs thudded off, settling into the swinging rhythm of a spurred run. If Don Ricardo entertained some hopeful idea of following through with his trick and playing it up to a smashing advantage, Osterberg's ready gun at his back had blocked it and sent him bolting for Mexico, gunless like Bishop.

THIRTEEN

The men out front were rushing to get into the house and shouting questions. At the door, Nunn, Dekker, and Colorado George stemmed the stampede.

"Hold off!" Nunn yelled. "Don't come trompin' in here in the dark—there's damage enough done!"

"What happened?"

"De Risa got hold o' Dyal's gun and went wild!" Dekker told them. "Cut loose at Bishop an' Dyal. Looked to me he shot the girl too. Owl—!"

"He grabbed a horse and got away!" Osterberg threw in a fearsome oath upon the departed Don Ricardo. "Don't anybody come in till we make a light." He stumbled into something and cursed again. "Got a match, Frank? Mine's all sweat-wet."

"You stink like a pig!" A note of almost hysterical elation edged Wittrock's voice. "This thing too much for you? Making you sweat?"

Bishop, rising from the floor, nudged Dyal. "Stay with Kerry!"

Dyal grunted, getting up. "I know my house better'n you! They're coming through the kitchen."

"All right, stay behind me."

"*You* stay behind *me!* And mind your big feet!"

Dyal crept quickly to the fireplace and from there to the short passage leading back to the kitchen. His carpet slippers had fallen off, and in his bare feet he made no sound. On tiptoe, Bishop had all he could do to keep up close to him.

"A match, Frank, a match! I keep bumping into the damn table!"

Osterberg's voice came from very near. A match scraped, and its weak light shone through the kitchen doorway on the left side of the passage. Bishop saw then that Dyal had the brass poker from the fireplace gripped upraised in both hands.

"That's the sink you're trying to get around," Wittrock said. "What's the matter with you, blind?"

"Blind in the dark, yeah. I ain't no cat. Did you hear something?"

"Sure. The men babbling. Come on!"

Wittrock stepped to the kitchen door, looking back impatiently, holding up the lighted match in his fingers. Some subtle sense of danger suddenly jerked his head around to Dyal and Bishop, pressed against the wall beside him. In the light of the match his pale face drained bone-white. He flicked his left hand and conjured the derringer into it.

Dyal chopped the brass poker at him. The doorframe was an obstacle, and either by mischance or intention he shaved Wittrock's face by an inch and struck the derringer from his hand. Wittrock sucked a breath and dodged back. The match blinked out. Bishop went in after him, hoping for a chance at Osterberg in the dark, but Wittrock called a warning.

"Look out! Broke my hand and got my pistol! They're—"

Bishop swung his fist at Wittrock's vague shape. It made contact, knocking Wittrock into the kitchen table, the table capsized with a crash of spilled dishes. Osterberg, alert by nature, must have backed up fast when the poker struck the derringer, for he fired one shot from the far end of the kitchen. His body darkened the outside doorway and was gone. Osterberg didn't trust his eyes in the dark.

The shot raised a new hubbub among the men at the front of the house. This time Nunn, Dekker, and Colorado George were among the questioners, until Osterberg barked, "Get round here to the back, some o' you—Bishop's trying to bust out!"

He reappeared crouched at the kitchen door, weaving from side to side, trying to peer in.

"Frank! Crawl this way if you can!"

Wittrock said bitterly on the floor, "If you had night-eyes or I had your gun—! He's standing near the table. Shoot high!"

Bishop changed position and ducked low, ahead of Osterberg's exploring shot. He backed out of the kitchen to the passage, the derringer in mind, and found Dyal gone. Broken crockery rattled. The derringer went off—*whump!*—in the front room and the hubbub became an uproar. He headed down the passage to the front room.

"Dyal, where are you?" In his hurry he grazed the swivel chair and it spun around, hit him in the rear, and banged into the desk.

"Told you to mind your big feet!" Dyal bobbed up, thrust-

107

ing something at him. "Here's a gun and shell belt for you, gunfighter! Nunn's. I got his rifle."

"And a shot left in the derringer?"

"Damn thing's no good. Missed Nunn a mile. I laid him out with the poker."

Bishop took the gun and belt, revising his opinion of the defenselessness of little old men in nightshirts. "Where's Kerry?"

"Behind the desk, or was till you sideswiped it. Anything more you want to know?"

"Yeah." Prickly old rooster. "Where are your crews?"

"Working cattle, where'd you think? Way off over the hills. Summer, ain't it? They're cowhands, not trigger-drifters!"

Bishop began a scorching retort. He cut it off, partly out of consideration for Kerry who had come around the desk to stand with them. It occurred to him that Dyal's snarling sarcasm cloaked desperate anxiety, rage, grief. Dyal had suffered much in his lifetime. This intolerable night should have broken him. He had learned that his wife, his beloved, estranged Anne, had been murdered. He had seen her murderer coldbloodedly arrange for his and his daughter's murder, and the peril of it stayed on to bedevil him.

"Get back down behind the desk," Bishop said to Kerry. He wasn't going to tell Dyal what to do. There were limits to his tolerance of tongue-lashing. "Somebody's liable to—"

A shot boomed enormously along the kitchen passage. Osterberg was clearing it for an advance.

"—liable to shoot," Bishop ended.

Wittrock's voice sounded in irritable query. "What did you shoot at? Nobody there. Anyway, all they got's my derringer."

"I can't see a damn—"

Bishop fired into the passage. He wasn't a whole lot better off than Osterberg when it came to seeing in the dark, and the flash of his own gun worsened the matter for the moment. He heard a noisy scrambling, but it was all boot-noise and he guessed his bullet hadn't made a profit.

"That wasn't any derringer. He's got a gun!"

"Get some of the men in here, then go round front and stir up the others. What do they think I'm paying them for? What's Nunn doing?"

Bishop blinked his eyes clear of the after-flash. He listened at the passage, while watching the dim outlines of the front windows and open door. Osterberg presently raised his voice.

"Jay! Jay Nunn!"

"He's lying on the floor in there," Dekker responded.

"They get his rifle an' gun?"

"Reckon so. Dunno what hit him. Somebody shot off a derringer, sounded like, but all it did was chip the door. We kinda jumped, and he—"

"Go help Frank," Osterberg said.

"De Risa crossed him up again, I guess, huh?"

"Ain't you smart! George?"

"Now look, Owl!" Colorado George complained. "My arm—"

"Frank wants a shotgun. Get him mine and some shells. Buckshot."

There was a short silence.

"Jeez—buckshot? The girl's in there!"

"That ain't your concern!" Osterberg spoke in the low monotone of restrained temper. "Frank's the boss and he knows what he wants. Where'd we be if he came out on the thin end o' this? We've showed our hands. No getting out of it now. You in any shape to go on the dodge?"

"You know I ain't."

"All right! We back him all the way! Take him the shotgun!"

Dyal had heard the exchange. He said with considerably less of his prickly roughness, "Bishop, we're finished if he comes in behind a shotgun! One night a packrat got in the kitchen, and he came downstairs and killed it in the dark. Threw the meat clever at it. How do we stop him?"

Bishop had no answer. He almost wished that Dyal hadn't brought up the subject so specifically. The prospect of being stalked in the dark by a cat-eyed creeper armed with a scattergun was a discomforting thought. A load of buckshot could tear a man to pieces. Sometimes it was best not to know the odds.

"How do we stop him?" Dyal repeated.

"Have to kill him." Bishop thought perhaps the old man's nerve was faltering, so he snapped, "Anything more you want to know?"

"Yeah!" Dyal flared. "How're we gonna do it?"

Osterberg called, "You fellers shy back there? Move up closer here, there's a job to finish!"

The men evidently were slow to obey, for he called again, grating the words out, "Move up here! You, Malone, come on! You scared of Bishop and an old mossback?"

"Hell, no, but we didn't take on to fight any girl!"

"Don't worry, she's safe upstairs. Come on!"

Bishop eased forward to the door, intent upon getting a shot at Osterberg. Without Osterberg to urge them on, the men, not eager to fire on a house that sheltered a girl, were apt to stand off and take no hand in it. It would at least lessen the danger from that quarter.

In the dark yard out front he spied a figure, its back toward the house, waving an upraised arm beckoningly. He sighted his gun at it and waited, not sure that it was Osterberg. It turned, came on, and still he held fire, wanting to make certain, trying to recognize the man's build and height, his manner of walking.

Dyal's rifle exploded a shell deafeningly close to his ear, startling him. He hadn't known that Dyal had followed him to the door with the same thought in mind, hadn't heard his bare feet on the floor.

The walking man dropped. Dyal said with grim satisfaction, levering a fresh shell into the breech, "That's Osterberg down, anyhow! What were you waiting for, Bishop?"

A gun blared along the front of the house, and they jumped back. Osterberg's voice rang out after the shot.

"Fellers, they got Malone!"

Malone must have filled the part of a leader, an acknowledged gun chief, or stood as a general favorite. The men came trampling forward, cursing in harsh, deep-throated voices.

Retreating with Dyal to the desk, Bishop said tightly, "Now you know what I was waiting for! To make sure it was Osterberg. You've played hell, killing their man!"

For once Dyal had no retort, and Bishop said to Kerry, "Upstairs is where you better be! Run!"

"No—they won't shoot while I'm here, will they?"

"Listen to them! They'll believe anything Osterberg tells them now. Run upstairs, I said!"

"I won't!"

"Bullheaded like your old man!" He picked her up bodily without further ado and stalked to the staircase. Dyal started to say something to him, and he rasped, "Don't you give me objections!"

"All I was saying was, you ought to be her father!"

"Oh." It wasn't any compliment to his age. Halfway up the stairs he turned Kerry loose. "Go on up and stay there! Bar your door and scream bloody murder if anybody starts to break it in!"

110

"I—"

"No argument, or I'll take the flat of my hand to you!" It sounded rough as a cob, and in an effort to taper it off into reasonableness he said, "Your father and I can't hustle so good with you underfoot. Do as I tell you like a good girl."

She ran on up the stairs, and he thought he heard her choke on a sob. He stood listening for a repetition of a sound in the kitchen passage, a creaking floorboard, but then the men out front raised a fresh outburst of anger for the late lamented Malone, so he gave up trying to distinguish one sound from another. It was wise to figure that Wittrock had the shotgun by now and was on his way to use it, taking advantage of the commotion. Dyal had unwittingly played into his hands with that premature rifle shot, and worsened a very bad jackpot. Too bad, but it couldn't be helped now. That was the kind of bobble to expect when a bullheaded cowman jumped the traces, and he took part of the blame on himself for letting it happen.

A man yelled, "Here's for Malone!" A gun flamed at the house. On its third shot others joined in.

They were punishing the house itself, as if it bore the guilt of Malone's death. Their indiscriminate blazing shattered the opened windows. Leaning over the banister, Bishop could see the flashes and the dark mass of men behind them. Dyal, down below, got off a shot in return.

Bishop called to him, "Hold it, Dyal! Wittrock's in—he'll spot your muzzle flash!"

He could just make out the entrance to the passage, a black rectangle in the darkness. Aiming his gun at it, he took off his hat, covered the muzzle with it, and fired through its crown. Distinctly, boot heels clacked a fast backstep, his speculative shot sending Wittrock to cover. Holding his gun and hat in place, he waited, estimating the time for Wittrock to make another move.

The shotgun roared a blinding streak. Below the staircase something metal clanged. Wittrock had figured pretty accurately the angle of Bishop's shot, but not the height it came from. Bishop fired. He heard Wittrock swear and scramble back. The absence of muzzle flash had him puzzled for the moment. He'd soon catch onto the trick, and his night eyes would search out the target.

Hunched low, Bishop crept down the stairs. To play the same trick three times running in the same spot went against

111

his gambling principles. It defied the laws of average and probability.

The men were coming up closer, urged on by Osterberg, by their anger, shooting at the house, the lack of return fire emboldening them to walk openly forward. They would have to stand right up to the windows and shoot in, Bishop decided, before he'd cut loose at them and betray his position to Wittrock.

As he crawled across the floor to the opposite wall he thought of Rico. No doubt Rico had foreseen this jackpot, or something of its kind, when he missed with his three shots and walked out. Knew he was only postponing the inevitable for a brief period. But his ruffled pride was preened. He had kept his code, such as it was, more or less intact. Blast him!

A head rose at one of the windows, bobbed down again, and Osterberg called, "Cool your shooters a minute, I want to talk to Frank."

Bishop crawled by the desk and came alongside Dyal crouched behind it. "Give me time to get near the passage," he whispered to him, "Then start firing."

"Muzzle flash, you said—"

"I want to draw Wittrock out."

He crawled on, close to the wall, making his slow advance more stealthily as the gunfire subsided. By sighting along the wall, he believed when he was near enough he'd be able to detect anything protruding from the entrance to the kitchen passage ahead. If he could get near enough, soon enough, if Wittrock didn't peer out and see him first.

"How's it go, Frank?" Osterberg sang out.

"Nothing so far," Wittrock answered from the passage. "Only a matter of time, though. I think Bishop pulled a hat trick on me."

"What kind?"

"Shot at me through his hat. Any idea where he is?"

"Could ask him. Hey, Bishop!" Osterberg paused. "Too smart to let out a peep! How 'bout we lower in a lantern on a pole, Frank?"

"He'd shoot it out. Might start a fire. Be seen for miles, a house this big."

"They'd come out or roast before that!"

Wittrock fell silent, evidently considering it. "That's true," he said. "I think I heard the girl run upstairs. All right, try a lantern. If it gets shot out and starts a fire—well, not our fault!"

112

His voice sounded very close. Bishop crawled another cautious yard, and stopped, hearing a muttering in the passage. There were others behind Wittrock. A hiss, and the muttering ceased. Wittrock was listening, perhaps sensing the nearness of the enemy. To move on closer without being heard was next to impossible. The slightest sound was audible in the hush. He wished some of the men would talk, cough, scrape their feet, anything. He wished he could let Dyal know to start shooting. What the hell delayed him? First he shot too quick, now he was too slow. Waiting for that lantern?

FOURTEEN

The report of the rifle came like a knife point scraped across his nerves. The next report didn't affect him, and the third was only a beat in time. Dyal was firing steadily, spacing his shots evenly between working the lever. It begot a deal of noise and confusion in front of the house, gunfire breaking out again and men calling to others to help somebody. Dyal had evidently scored a hit or two. Perhaps he had been waiting for targets, disliking to waste ammunition.

From Bishop's perspective the passage entrance was a thin line flush in the wall against which he crouched. It broke shape between one instant and the next. He hardly saw the change take place, it came so swiftly. It was suddenly there, a bulge halfway up its length, motionless, nothing much about it to indicate its menace as a killer about to discharge two loads of buckshot.

He fired twice, the second shot fast after the other.

The bulge toppled outward, enlarging, becoming the shape of a man. It made no sound until it bumped the floor and the shotgun clattered and slid a little way. A voice in the passage exclaimed, "Gahdamn!" and Colorado George asked with a note of disbelief, "He got him? Him? Frank? *Ho*-lee——! Hey, Owl! Owl!"

He made the short distance in three strides, and emptied his gun of its last two shells into the dark passage. Colorado George abruptly quit yelling for Owl. Men plunging out through the kitchen made a racket that was agreeable to his ears. He picked up the shotgun. He ran a hand over Wittrock's coat, located a pocketful of shotgun shells, and transferred them to his own pocket.

"Now, by damn!"

Dyal, not sure who had got shot in the dark, and having spent the shells in his rifle, asked, "What you crowing about? They bring a lantern——"

"Suits me if they all bring lanterns!"

"And burn the house down on us?"

"Let 'em try!"

114

A shotgun didn't stand in his favor. Its spreading pattern of pellets was apt to hit too many marks and bring about unfortunate complications, while on the receiving end a man armed with a respectable handgun couldn't count on his skill against it. He granted, however, that there were times when it had its uses, occasions when no man need feel shame to unlimber it against other than wild game. Especially when badly outnumbered and bereft of any other workable weapon. Such as now.

For a start he fired a load that flayed the low sill of the window where Osterberg had bobbed up his head, on the chance that Osterberg might be raising an ear to listen. Two men farther out yelped, one claiming a slug in his leg, the other a nicked ankle. His next load went out the door on speculation. He broke open the shotgun, ejected, reloaded, snapped it closed.

Osterberg shouted, "Frank!" He sounded anxious, as if the strain of guessing in the dark was wearing him down. "George! What's going on in there? Dammit, Frank nigh shot *me!*"

A man running around the house answered, "Bishop dropped Frank and took his scattergun!"

"No! George?"

"Got another bullet."

Bishop spoke up. "Take your men and pull out, Owl, there's nothing here for you!"

Dyal crawled forward to him. He asked, "That right you've killed Frank Wittrock?"

"Had to."

"Don't apologize," Dyal grunted. He was thinking, Bishop supposed, of his murdered wife, Anne. Of all the evil that Frank Wittrock had brought to Hatchet.

Presently, Osterberg said outside, "All right, Bishop. I got to pull out. All right! But I won't leave much behind here. Me an' Frank worked three years on this. Three years, taking the old man's tongue-lashings and sweating for his lousy pay! You think I'd leave it stand, no satisfaction at all?"

"You're a stinking-bad loser, Owl."

"Dead right I am!" Osterberg raised his voice. "Fellers, give it hell! You dancing to their tune? Got Malone, didn't they? Got Frank Wittrock, Colorado George . . . Give it hell, I say!"

By his power to command he forced on a renewed burst

115

of gunfire. It slackened shortly, and he shouted, "Get on up to the windows and shoot in!"

"How 'bout that scattergun?"

"He shot it off twice, didn't he? It's empty!"

"You guar'ntee that?" The question was skeptical.

"Sure I do! And I'll give a hundred dollars each to the first two men in the door!"

"They'll earn it, they get their heads blown off!" the skeptic observed, but Osterberg's cash offer aroused some discussion among the men.

Dyal, hugging the floor beside Bishop, made to take hold of the shotgun. Bishop jerked it out of his reach and moved nearer to the door to listen to the talkers. Among that hired jumble of hardcases, gunhands, fighters for daily wages, there were pretty sure to be a couple of knotheads who'd talk themselves into making a stab at any dumb play for money. Osterberg had surely heard the closing click of the shotgun, crouched down as he was against the front of the house. He knew it was reloaded, else he wouldn't wait to come in. He'd come in right after its two barrels emptied again, on the dot.

Close to the door, Bishop rose to his feet and peered out at the shadowy figures in the yard. They were debating Osterberg's offer, some sounding tempted, wiser heards arguing against it, pointing out that Colorado George had taken a supply of shells around to Frank Wittrock and the odds were that Bishop had got them along with the shotgun.

Osterberg called to them, "I'll double it! Two hundred dollars apiece!"

Bishop swore under his breath, giving up hope that the wiser heads would prevail. Osterberg could raise his offer to whatever amount lured the takers, knowing he'd never be called on to make it good. Dead men couldn't collect, even if he had it to pay out. But his bid was too tempting for money-hungry gunhands to resist.

They stopped talking. One of them sang out, "Deal me in! You, Stan?"

"You bet!"

Two figures detached themselves from the huddle. They paced forward, slowly at first, then hastening as others began an advance to overtake them. The movement threatened to become a race to the house. Watching them, Bishop drew a spare shell from his pocket and held it ready.

He tipped the shotgun low and fired off one barrel directly ahead of them at the hard-packed ground. Ricochet buckshot sprayed the leading pair. He used the noise of their pained yells to cover the sound of swiftly ejecting the spent shell and slipping in the spare. Quietly closing the shotgun, he immediately fired a second shot.

Between his two shots he had allowed only the briefest space of time. It matched the momentary pause of a shooter swinging onto his second target. It drew Osterberg in a rush from his crouched cover against the house. Sure that the shotgun was fired empty, intent on giving not an instant for it to be reloaded, he plunged in through the door with a gun in each hand.

He met the blaring discharge of the third shot at close range. It punched him back and he fell outside. The front of his shirt smoldered.

A stunned silence lengthened, until Simon Dyal exclaimed unbelievingly, "What? How'd you get three shells in a double-barrel? It can't be done!"

"That's what he'd like to know, if he lived!"

Bishop stepped to a window, reloading. He commenced firing steadily, aiming low for the buckshot to bounce and scatter wide. The men fell back from the cutting hail, mindful of their eyes, cursing him, cursing Osterberg for guaranteeing an empty shotgun. It was like driving off an onrush of belligerent bulls, and cost him six shells to clear the front yard of them. He felt in his pocket, counting three remaining shells.

Dyal said in immense relief, "Got 'em on the run!"

"You've been home too long," Bishop commented. Three shells and two in the breech. Buckshot, good within forty yards at most. If they brought up rifles . . .

"You mean it's made me soft? *Me?*"

"Makes you feel safe too soon. Do they sound like they're quitting?"

They had gathered beyond the yard to pitch haphazard shots back at the house. In the moonless night they couldn't see what they were hitting and were too sore to care. Uncertain of what had befallen Osterberg, he had dropped so fast, and clinging to the persuasion that they had back wages due, some of them shouted demands about who was going to pay them off.

Dyal bellowed at them, "Osterberg's down! So's Wittrock! Get off Hatchet, you scum!"

An angry uproar responded. "You don't know their kind,"

Bishop told him. "I guess their kind wasn't around in your day. There's no place left for 'em in Texas, and they're so broke a ten-dollar bill looks as big as a saddle blanket. Up in Cedar Valley I bought their kind for forty a month."

"To fight friends o' mine! Decent cattlemen! You any better'n them?"

"Don't rattle your horns at me, old-timer! Your decent cattlemen needed a checkrein. Maybe you do, too!"

He listened to a voice loudly insisting that there was cash in the house, that the plain thing to do was rush the house for it, take the blood money that was rightly coming to them.

"That right, Dyal? Cash in the house?"

"I got cash on hand, sure. Damned if I pay it to those scum, though! It goes for something else."

"If they rush us front and back . . ." Bishop left the rest unsaid. They had taken painful damage, lost their leaders, got cut off from their pay. Their blood was up and they could figure that the supply left of shotgun shells was running low. The lure of cash in the house was gaining more and more shouting supporters for an attack. Scum they might be, from Dyal's outlook, but to underestimate them in their savage mood was a foolhardy mistake.

The racket died down to a muttering that to Bishop's ears carried the sharp give-and-take of a rapid parley preceding action. In the respite he heard Kerry on the stairs, coughing and sneezing in the powdersmoke-fouled air.

"Go back!" he called to her. "We're not through!"

"I heard—" A sneeze intruded.

"Never mind what you heard! Go back!"

"But I heard upstairs, from my window—" She sneezed again, and gasped in exasperation, "Oh, damn!"

He shook his head. Stubborn, stubborn. Old Man Dyal all over again, damning any obstacle that got in the way. Her mother, that real refined lady, would have washed her mouth out with soap.

"Dyal, make her mind."

"You do it!" Dyal retorted; but he said to her, "Kerry, those scum are about to make another try. That what you heard from your window?"

"We heard it too," Bishop put in. "I could hear better if you'd keep quiet."

"No!" She flew pattering down the stairs. "What I heard was something else. Why don't you listen?"

"I'm trying to."

It occurred to him that perhaps she had, in fact, been able to hear better from an upstairs window. He stood at the door, head bent. The muttering had entirely ceased, replaced by dwindling sounds of movement. Merging with those sounds rose another, a far-off undertone, growing to a steady rumble.

"What d'you make of it, Dyal?"

"Riders, coming this way."

"Not my cowhands. Wrong direction. More of Osterberg's scum?"

In the near distance, beyond the oak windbreaks, saddles creaked faintly, men spoke in quick tones, and horse hoofs thudded.

"Our scum's gone to meet 'em," Dyal said.

Bishop drew his brows down. "I think you're wrong," he said, but his frown had nothing to do with that.

He disliked, suddenly and without much defensible reason, Dyal's repeated use of the term *scum*. It was all right for gunslingers to recognize grades among themselves, class distinction being won by talent or lost for lack of it. An ace could look down his nose at a deuce. It wasn't all right for an outsider to make free at smearing muck at the trade, nor at any part of it. Some of those dodgers had likely come down in the world, been proud and choosy, before Texas law made lowly gun tramps of them. Besides, muck was liable to splatter.

They stood listening to the oncoming riders. Osterberg's men had either split up and scattered, or gone circling off around the hills, for the advancing party never changed rhythm. Sheriff's posse, Bishop guessed, rounding in on Hatchet, minutes too late for a fight, minutes too soon for him to reach a horse.

He sighed faintly, too bone-tired to try a run for it, wishing now that he had taken a less rough tongue toward Kerry, wishing that he had taken some small pains not to rub Simon Dyal the wrong way. Dyal could tell any tale that suited him, be believed, throw him to the wolves. He hadn't much faith left in big Texas cattlemen. Nor in little cattlemen, since Cedar Valley.

The riders streamed through the oak trees and on into the yard, pulling up before the house. A posse, definitely, stiff with deputies. Direct and businesslike. They grunted clipped comments concerning the shattered windows, bullet-riddled

119

walls, the dark shapes lying near the door. Needing no order, half of the posse split off, swung smartly around the house.

"Mr. Dyal! You theah?" And that was County Sheriff Sutter himself, legging down off his horse, his voice steel hard.

Dyal lighted the lamp. "I'm here."

"Miss Kerry theah?"

"She's here."

"Bishop theah?"

"Dammit, man, come in and see!"

FIFTEEN

Men lined the windows. They kept their faces empty of expression at the sight of Dyal in a nightshirt, Kerry in dancehall dress. Men's boots clopped in the kitchen. County Sheriff Sutter stepped through the front door.

He touched his hat to Kerry. "Glad to see you home again, Miss Kerry!" He took his eyes off her dress, stuck a thumb over his shoulder. "That's Osterberg. Who killed him?"

Sutter's eyes cut past him to the entrance of the kitchen passage. "And there's Frank Wittrock, by God! Who killed—"

"Bishop."

A deputy entered from the rear, stepping over Wittrock's body. "Colorado George's in the kitchen. He's dead."

"Who—"

"Bishop," said Dyal.

Sutter looked at him. "You've had a rough time." He looked at Bishop, at the shotgun in his hands. "You're a killer!"

"I guess I am," Bishop said, "this night." He shook his head at Sutter's motion at him to lay down the shotgun. "No, this is all I've got. I don't like going naked." As he said it, without any humor, it came to him that without a gun of some kind he did feel naked. He was that far a gunfighter, all the way.

Kerry moved to him, stood before him, saying firmly to Sutter, "He brought me home, fought for me—I owe him my life!"

Sutter ran his eyes over her dress, her tumbled hair, her face. She was blocking his raised gun. "You've changed a lot since you've been away! I was down at Forks looking into a shoot-out there. They say you were in the bar with Bishop and—"

"Quit that!" Dyal interrupted him roughly. His bloodshot eye flared open and his thick lower lip jutted out. Again the ridiculous composite of nightshirt and outsize hat counted for

121

nothing. He was a tough old rawhide, forceful, domineering. "It's my daughter you're talking to, Sutter!"

"I'm in no danger of forgetting it, *Mister* Dyal! As sheriff of this county it's my right to ask her where and what—"

"I don't give a damn where she was or what she did, she's still a lady and my daughter!" Dyal thundered. "If she's changed, it's for the better! Now drop it! Turn your strictly official attention to the shoot-out we've had here tonight with a pack of scummy gunmen!"

"Where are they?"

"They just left."

"Bishop bring 'em?"

"Hell, no! Osterberg hired 'em. For Wittrock." Dyal pointed unemotionally at the body by the passage entrance. "Yes, Wittrock! Against Hatchet. He'd have murdered Kerry and me, like he murdered my wife . . ." Emotion then caught up with him. He cleared his throat with an enormous bark. "Tell you about it later. I need a drink. Bottles in that cabinet there, Bishop."

"Wish you'd told me sooner."

Sutter's eyes followed Bishop to the cabinet. "You might tell me a little more now, Mr. Dyal. I've got to know where he stands. About the fight. Did you and Bishop—"

Opening the cabinet, Bishop paused for Dyal's reply. He heard Dyal say, "It was all his. Or mostly." He chose a full bottle of Kentucky bourbon, sour mash, aged, high proof, uncorked it and carried it to Dyal.

Gravely, with a touch of ceremony, Dyal raised it. "To your health, Mr. Bishop." He drank straight from the bottle and handed it back.

"And to yours, Mr. Dyal." Bishop followed suit.

Sutter rubbed his nose, gazing from one to the other. "As sheriff of this county I get less information than Paddy's pig!" he complained. "I was told in Forks that there was a raid on Hatchet. That's all. Just that. A raid on Hatchet. A Mexican rode in and said so. Stranger to me. I wouldn't have known that much—and how he knew . . ." He turned to the onlooking possemen. "Where's the Mexican. Send him in."

There seemed to be some slight altercation outside, a shy diffidence on the part of the Mexican, earnest urging on the part of the possemen. Presently, Don Ricardo de Risa paced sedately into the big room.

He glanced at Bishop, bottle in hand and Kerry at his elbow. He swept off his sombrero and bowed to Kerry. When he straightened up he gazed at Simon Dyal. Except for his eyes, which held a tiny glimmer of inquiry, his face was impassive.

Sutter asked him, "How did you know there was a raid on here, amigo? I haven't had time to wonder till now."

"I was passing by, and became, er—embroiled—"

"He helped out," Dyal said.

Don Ricardo inclined his head. "Happy to have been of some small service," he murmured modestly.

"I'll tell you later about that, too," Dyal promised Sutter. He met Don Ricardo's level gaze. "Tomorrow."

Don Ricardo edged unobtrusively over to Bishop. "Mecca tomorrow!" he whispered. "Or I should say, Mexico tomorrow!"

"You took a chance, coming back. Why?"

"Curiosity. To see if my little trick had done any good. Also, it was probably the only opportunity I'll ever have of riding with a Texas sheriff's posse."

"I wouldn't bet on it," Bishop muttered. "Sutter's got his eye on you!"

Sutter was staring hard at Don Ricardo in the light of the lamp. A couple of his deputies also evinced solemn interest. "Haven't I seen your face somewhere before?" Sutter demanded.

"I very much doubt it," Don Ricardo disclaimed, slipping a hand back toward the shotgun. Bishop let him have the whiskey bottle instead. "Mine is a common type of face— you see it here, there, everywhere."

"I don't agree, not a bit! What's your name?"

"Luciano Diego Santiago Aguilar de Chavez y Castillo."

"Whoo!" said a deputy. "Where's the others?"

"I vouch for, m'mm, Louie Castillo," Bishop put in. "He's a *ranchero muy grande*. Big cattleman in Mexico."

By Sutter's dubious expression, an avouchment from Bishop represented less than a perfect recommendation. Casually, Bishop brought up the shotgun, scratching his thumbnail at a rust spot on the trigger guard. Sutter's eyes flashed. Don Ricardo raised the bottle and took a drink.

"Leave him be," Dyal said. "He helped out, I tell you! That right, Kerry?"

"Yes, he—helped."

"That ought to be enough for you, Sutter. If you don't mind, I'd like you to go now. We've been through a lot here, and I'm feeling my years. Thanks for coming."

Sutter's eyes stayed on the shotgun. "We'll clean up around here before we go." Nodding at the shotgun, he added, "That thing's made business for the undertaker."

"It wasn't his choice," Dyal said. "A man's got to make do with what comes to his hand."

"So I see!"

The possemen carried out the remains of Frank Wittrock. Don Ricardo followed them, Bishop behind him. At the door he stopped, looked back at Kerry, sighed, put a finger to his lips and flipped it at her. Hurrying to his horse, he swung into the saddle and glanced about at the possemen watching him.

"Rogue, they're not satisfied—and I haven't a gun! Will you—?"

"Go ahead!"

Dyal called from the house, "Bishop, I want a word with you."

"Be with you in a minute."

He saw Don Ricardo off to a flying start, waited to make sure that nobody set out after him, and walked back to the house. Passing Sutter at the door, he handed him the shotgun. "This belongs with Osterberg's things. If you find a pair of black-handled guns, they're mine."

He went on in, Sutter staring after him while unloading the shotgun.

Simon Dyal was alone, sitting at the desk. "Kerry's gone upstairs to change her dress," he said. "How'd she come to be wearing that scented get-up?"

Bishop explained. The old man drummed his fingers on the desk.

"That Mexican! Known him long?"

"Years, off and on." Bishop paused to search for the right words. "He didn't harm your daughter, nor let harm come to her. He loves her, or thinks he does, but—well, I want you to know she got through without harm. Somehow."

But, he mused privately, it was touch-and-go there for a while.

Dyal nodded, his wide-open eye fixed shrewdly on Bishop's face. "You didn't have to tell me, but thanks."

Bishop was silent, and the old man went on, "I don't know how much she thinks of you. I'm afraid it's too much."

"Afraid?"

"Look, Bishop. Look at her picture there. You see a girl who's unhappy, distrustful. That's how her mother looked when she moved to the other house. Why did I let this house

124

go to pot? With them gone, I hated it! They were all I cared for in the world. Last year, after her mother died . . ." Dyal turned his head abruptly before resuming.

"Kerry came back to live with me. Only because she had to. I hoped we'd get onto a good footing, but no. She was more unhappy than ever, more distrustful. We couldn't get together. It got worse. She distrusted *me!* Sometimes I caught her looking at me like I was a monster. I gave up. It hurts too much when you love somebody who hates you."

Bishop absently examined the shot-ruined crown of his hat. "Wittrock got in his work there," he mentioned. "Dropped hints. Pretended sympathy for her. Then that letter. And now? How about now?"

"The future, you mean," Dyal corrected him. "She's come back alive. She was only half alive, and she's come back full alive, glowing like any healthy girl with a healthy mind should! She's come back to me, her father! She's my daughter again! That's what I mean by the future—a good future for us both."

"And some day you'll hear her laughter."

"Eh? Why, yes. We'll do this house over, top to bottom. New furniture, curtains and drapes, everything—let her take charge of that. We'll give parties, dances. Music and wine, by God, and bright lights all through the house? She's got a lot of living to make up for. A lot of playing to catch up on. She'll be the belle of the county!" The old man got to his feet. "You see why I'm afraid she thinks too much of you?"

Bishop slowly nodded. "I don't belong in that future." He felt cold inside, and older by years.

"You'd rob her of it." Dyal struck him on the shoulder, a clumsy tap intended as fraternal. "Not that you'd want to, but you couldn't help it. She's entitled to be young and gay and free. Her future belongs to her. Where would you fit in?"

"Nowhere." Nowhere here, his mind said. Nowhere in Texas, present or future.

"Don't go yet," Dyal stopped him. "We got another minute or two, friend . . ."

He was walking to the door when Kerry ran down the stairs. Passing her father, she patted his arm quickly in a gesture that was wholly natural, an unself-conscious expression of affection, and hastened on to Bishop.

"You're not leaving?" Her eyes were wide. She wore a blue dress like the girl in the portrait, but she was a different girl.

125

"There are some things," he said with difficulty, "that I've got to go and straighten out."

"But you'll come back?" Her hands reached up to his shoulders. She was very serious in her question. "You must come back, you must, Rogue!"

He drew a deep breath and let it out. "Yes," he lied, "I'll come back." Who was it said that the swift stroke of the knife was kindest. Truer was the saying that time healed all wounds. She was so young.

"Soon? Make it be soon, Rogue!"

He kissed her lightly, like an older brother. "As soon as my way is clear." And that would be never.

She laughed softly. "There's nothing here on Hatchet in your way! I'll be waiting . . ."

They came together on the road south of Bandera, both having avoided that hostile town. An exchange of nods was their only greeting.

"Your guns," Bishop said, handing them over, and Don Ricardo thankfully holstered them. Wordless, they rode on, each sunk in his own thoughts.

At last Don Ricardo, incurably romantic, sighed and said pensively, "How lovely she was! I shall long dream of her eyes, her lips, her hair, her ravishing—"

"And the money she'll inherit some day!" Bishop put in brutally.

"You have the soul of an ox! Adorable Kerry, *mi corazón!* I could have made her happy. She would have blossomed, a rare rose in my tender care, learning love and laughter—"

"I heard her laugh."

"As my bride—yes, I would have married her, gladly! As my beautiful young bride, Princess of the Hill Country, I the Prince, heirs-apparent to Hatchet, as it were—"

"How about Old Man Dyal as a father-in-law?"

Don Ricardo blinked rapidly, jolted back down to earth from lofty heights. *"Sangre del santos,* you spoil everything for me! Speaking of money, we lost high stakes there."

"Collected ten thousand in ransoms, didn't you? And he paid me the five thousand we agreed on. Had it ready in the house. We did all right," Bishop said harshly.

Some day, after the waiting ran its course, when the house was joyous and life was good, some tall young Texan would win her heart and hand, damn him. She'd be a bride, a wife, a mother, perhaps once in a blue moon pausing in her busy

126

rounds to recollect an old infatuation, smiling at its foolishness, grateful that he never came back.

"I turn off here," Bishop announced abruptly. "Figure to head for New Mexico—Pecos, or down to Silver City. Maybe on to Arizona."

"Arizona?" Don Ricardo nodded consideringly. "Some good towns there. Tombstone, Nogales, Tucson—heavy games and light law, eh? I may try Arizona myself, by way of Mexico. Or perhaps even California. We're played out in these parts, *compadre*."

"We sure are." Bishop lifted his reins.

"*Adiós*, Rogue! If we meet again, God forbid, may it bring us no regrets!"

"Yeah. S'long, Rico."

No regrets. This time, for sure, it was farewell to Texas.

L(eonard) L(ondon) Foreman was born in London, England in 1901. He served in the British army during the Great War, prior to his emigration to the United States. He became an itinerant, holding a series of odd jobs in the western States as he traveled. He began his writing career by introducing his most widely known and best-loved character, Preacher Devlin, in "Noose Fodder" in *Western Aces* (12/34), a pulp magazine. Throughout the mid thirties, this character, a combination gunfighter, gambler, and philosopher, appeared regularly in *Western Aces*. Near the end of the decade, Foreman's Western stories began appearing in Street & Smith's *Western Story Magazine*, where the pay was better. Foreman's first Western novels began appearing in the 1940s, largely historical Westerns such as *Don Desperado* (1941) and *The Renegade* (1942). The *New York Herald Tribune* reviewer commented on *Don Desperado* that "admirers of the late beloved Dane Coolidge better take a look at this. It has that same all-wool-and-a-yard-wide quality." Foreman continued to write prolifically for the magazine market as long as it lasted, before specializing exclusively for the book trade with one of his finest novels, *Arrow in the Dust* (1954) which was filmed under this title the same year. Two years earlier *The Renegade* was filmed as *The Savage* (Paramount, 1952), the two are among several films based on his work. Foreman's last years were spent living in the state of Oregon. Perhaps his most popular character after Preacher Devlin was Rogue Bishop, appearing in a series of novels published by Doubleday in the 1960s. George Walsh, writing in *Twentieth Century Western Writers*, said of Foreman: "His novels have a sense of authority because he does not deal in simple characters or simple answers." In fact, most of his fiction is not centered on a confrontation between good and evil, but rather on his characters and the changes they undergo. His female characters, above all, are memorably drawn and central to his stories.